SHADOWS OF PROPHECY

BY D.A. GODWIN

Guardian's Prophecy
Book One: Eyes of the Blind
Book Two: Hunter's Moon
Book Three: Weaponforger
Book Four: New Moon Rising
Book Five: Shadows of Prophecy

SHADOWS OF PROPHECY

GUARDIAN'S PROPHECY: BOOK FIVE

By

D.A. Godwin

CONTENTS

One of the most enjoyable elements of writing has been discovering how drastically wrong my notions of the future can be.

When I first began working on *Eyes of the Blind*, the story (I hesitate to name it an actual plot at that time) centered around two brothers and the parallel paths they would follow towards the same ending. As such, we spent a good deal of time getting to know both Tormjere and Eljorn. Each set off to follow their own destinies—one as a ranger and the other as an itinerant monk—and save the world together through their complementary blend of skills. Shalindra was to fulfill an important but supporting role, and Enna had yet to make herself known. It was a solid concept, and one which was shaping up to be a rather fun adventure.

Tormjere, however, had other plans.

When I was roughly a third of the way through the mishmash of words that would grow to be the first draft, I stumbled upon the climactic finale of book three. This came as quite a shock, because one book seemed a daunting enough mountain to climb. Yet there I sat with four beginnings and four endings, and a lot of rewriting to do.

And those changes began with, literally, the very first word.

Eljorn had always been the focus of the opening scene since he would be the first to leave. I stubbornly clung to that perspective all the way until I sent the manuscript off to my editor, who, after taking my money and rolling her eyes (in that order, lest I become indignant and refuse to pay her), promptly affirmed what everyone else had been telling me for years: it's not the best idea to lead off a new series from a secondary character's point of view. And so it was that *Eyes of the Blind* became, completely, Tormjere's story.

But I never quite forgot how it was meant to begin, and neither did Eljorn. While his path would carry him far away before bringing him back, the road he chose for himself remained very interesting…

The Sixfold Path

Eljorn stepped smoothly across the slippery rocks in the creek, making his way to a mossy boulder half-submerged near the middle. His bare feet left wet footprints on the granite as he climbed to the top and sat, facing upstream, as was his habit. He closed his eyes, listening to the muted roar of cold water pouring over countless stones as it tumbled down the mountain. Sunlight filtered through the falling leaves to warm his face, perfectly balancing the chill of the early morning.

He took a deep breath of the moist, fragrant air and settled himself, assuming a serene countenance that was mature beyond his years. Though he had no real claim to it, he had always considered this to be *his* rock, in *his* creek. It had been here, solid and unmoving, for his entire life—all thirteen summers of it— offering wisdom and comfort while asking nothing in return. Here, in this place, he was at peace.

If only everything was so simple, he thought.

After today, it would all be different. The soothing sounds of running water offered a gentle counsel that helped to ease his mind.

Different didn't mean bad. He relaxed, letting his thoughts drift.

The coldness of the stone had barely worked its way through his loose tunic when an almost imperceptible change in the pattern of echoes announced an end to his solitude. He opened one eye and glanced toward the shore to see his older brother, Tormjere. Hair as dark and wild as his eyes perfectly framed the scowl on his face, and his arms were crossed defensively. It was a look Eljorn knew all too well.

"Put away the frown, brother," he called, almost shouting to be heard over the rush of the water. "This day is too nice for unhappiness!"

Poking fun at his brother when he was in such a serious mood always garnered a good response, and today was no exception.

"You're going to spend the rest of your life meditating in a cave somewhere," Tormjere said, "and this is what you do with your last day of freedom?" He crossed the wet stones and climbed up beside Eljorn, shouldering him to the side so they would both fit.

"I did feed the dogs this morning," Eljorn pointed out, shifting his weight to prevent himself sliding off.

"It was your turn anyway."

Their family owned the only kennel in the valley, or "the cove" as those who lived there called it, and both siblings had helped with the business since an early age.

"Speaking of which, where's Blackwolf?" Eljorn asked. Tormjere was rarely without his favorite dog, especially here in the woods.

Tormjere's frown finally cracked. "He managed to get into what was to be tonight's supper, and Father locked him up for a while."

Eljorn chuckled at the thought of the sometimes-troublesome animal stealing their food.

Talking about the animals always made Tormjere smile, but today he gave Eljorn no chance to further lighten the conversation. "What will you do for fun?" he asked.

Eljorn had asked himself the same question so many times that his answer felt like he was repeating a mantra: "I'm sure something will present itself." He truly believed that it would and was willing to take the uncertain future on faith.

"Doubt it. They'll make you cut your hair you know."

"Only if I'm accepted," he said, forcing a laugh. "It will not be missed."

In an attempt to hide his own doubts, he turned his gaze to the multicolored leaves slowly falling through the air. That final act— the cutting of his hair—would come only at the end of his initiation, but the fear of somehow failing the first year and being sent home weighed heavily upon him. No matter how certain of this choice he was, the thought that he might not be made for the life of a wandering monk continued to nag at him. It was unproductive to reach for what might be when he had so much waiting right in front of him, and so he dismissed the notion as just another daydream.

"What *will* you miss?" his brother asked.

"This," Eljorn answered without hesitation, "and Mother and Father, and the dogs, and you." He looked up the creek, absently following its path through the trees. "But I want to do this—it just feels right."

Tormjere gave no response this time, and Eljorn could add nothing that would make it any better. Their family was about to be split apart, and no matter how sound the reasoning behind his decision, it was going to be hard on all of them. The brothers sat in silence for a time, each trying to control their emotions. Eljorn was torn between excitement about his commitment and dread at what he would be giving up to pursue it. The rewards of a monastic life were sure to be plenty, yet even without them he felt a need to answer this calling.

"We should head back," Tormjere finally said. "They were spotted coming down the pass, so it won't be long now." He rose and crossed the rocks to the shore, where he stopped, waiting expectantly.

Eljorn followed reluctantly. 'Keep your eyes on the path ahead,' that was the axiom. It made sense for any number of situations, but as he took one last look at the creek, he wondered if he would ever see this place again.

* * *

That afternoon, the village was abuzz with excitement. Every other year, the Toushin monks would visit villages and towns throughout the Kingdom, searching for new applicants. The Brotherhood was respected far and wide for their charity and fairness, and it was considered an honor if a family member was accepted into their ranks. As Eljorn stood nervously with his family, he could only hope that he would be judged worthy of their high standards and justify his own family's pride in his choice.

The procession arrived with the customary trappings of ceremony, preceded by pounding drums and flags in their traditional browns and yellows. Their quest must have departed the monastery weeks earlier with only a handful of monks, yet none of the robed men appeared road weary. Eljorn suddenly realized that he had no idea where the monastery was or how long the journey would actually take. Kenzing was clearly not their first stop, as they had collected several dozen new applicants—or *dimnants*, as they were known. Given the forlorn looks on some of their faces, he judged that many would not make it through the long walk back to the monastery, and fewer still would remain after the demands of the first year. Followers of Toush led a difficult life, but Eljorn found the rigor of it appealing.

In spite of those daunting challenges, there was hope and fortitude in many of the dimnants' eyes. Eljorn forced his shoulders to relax and slowed his breathing. In the next village, *he* would be the one accepting food and water from the crowd. The realization made the expensive lunch of roast his mother had prepared earlier all the more special.

As the procession reached the common field, the drums stopped, and an older monk dressed in yellow and orange walked slowly towards the center of the open space. Unlike larger towns, Kenzing had no official speaking platform. The monk, however, walked with purpose towards a particular patch of earth as if it had been placed there for just such an occasion.

"Is that the Mantrin?" Tormjere asked in a low voice.

"No," Eljorn said, "the Mantrin would be in red and gold, but he never walks the Journey of Entry. He has too many other responsibilities. The orange means he's one of the Suman. They report directly to the Mantrin."

Despite Eljorn's best efforts, his stomach was dancing about as the moment drew ever closer.

The Suman monk turned to face them from his chosen place, and the crowd fell silent. "Those who walk in the footsteps of

Toush bring a question to the Kingdom of Actondel," he said in a loud, clear voice. "May we speak?"

It was a formal request. Anyone who wanted to address such an assembly was expected to first gain the permission of the local lord. Since the village had no officially appointed steward, such formalities fell to the commander of the garrison as the most senior representative of the crown.

Sir Warron, standing tall at the front of the crowd with the green-and-gold tabard of the King's Army draped over his chain hauberk, had occupied that position forever.

"All those who bring peace may speak and be welcome," he replied with the corresponding formality.

"We come in the name of Toush, the Great Thinker," the monk began, "he who sits in contemplation, guiding the choices that we make as we walk our path through life. There are many paths which may be chosen, each with their own trials and rewards. Some are easy and may be trod without care. Others are difficult and should be traveled with caution. Toush, recognizing that knowledge of what lies ahead makes the chosen path easier to walk, established the Six Pillars of Service and vowed to walk his own path six times over so that he might learn fully from each."

As the speech continued, Eljorn found himself swept up in the monk's words. A desire to travel to distant lands, to make a difference in the lives of not just a few but many, *that* was what he truly desired. It was as if the monk were speaking directly to him, clarifying the jumble of his desires into a single concise purpose. He snuck a glance at his brother, whose selfless act of bravery years ago against the troll had unknowingly inspired him to take these steps. They had grown up together, shared secrets and adventures and dreams, and now that comradery would be gone. Eljorn's emotions continued to be turbulent until the Suman monk reached the point he had been eagerly awaiting for so long.

"All those who would devote their lives to Toush and join us in our eternal quest along the Sixfold Path, please come forward."

It was time.

Eljorn hugged his mother, doing his best to ignore the tears in her eyes, and then his father gave him a hearty slap on the back. He expected something witty from Tormjere, but his brother's mouth was clamped shut. Eljorn met his brother's eyes, and he knew they were both feeling the same things. Their family would be apart for the first time in either of their lives, and the dreams they had shared as children were being swept aside by the call of manhood. Each put their hands on the other's shoulders, and Eljorn vowed that nothing would ever come between their love for each other. With a final smile to them all, he turned and walked away to join the other dimnants.

There was no telling where destiny would lead his path, but with Toush as his guide, he was certain that it was meant to begin right here.

Introduction to
"An Unwelcome Apprentice"

It was very early on during the writing of *Eyes of the Blind* that I made a conscious decision to keep the story directly with, or very close to, our heroes. What was unknown to them would be equally unknown to you, and thus the mysteries they were forced to confront could be unraveled together.

I ignored many suggestions to alter that stance, to enhance the impending danger by jumping across time and space to reveal what the "bad guys" were doing. That is a storytelling mechanism so ensconced in the genre that perhaps only the obligatory "wizard's introduction" might be more prominent.

But I wanted something different.

I wanted to maintain that sense of uncertainty, to explore new places at the speed our heroes travelled, and to allow every turn of the page to reveal a new mystery.

The world Tormjere travelled through is as vast and varied as our own, with millions of people and an untold number of momentous events in motion at any given time. Even the villains pursued their objectives with purpose and conviction, though their motivations were often obscured by the limitations of our heroes' awareness.

Herein is revealed one such tale, that of two wizards who unwillingly found themselves rushing headlong towards a decision that would alter history.

An Unwelcome Apprentice

Felzig tugged on his formal jacket, straining against the intentional snugness of the richly embellished, deep red material as he drew it closed around his thin frame. His long fingers fastened the golden buttons with the same meticulous precision he exhibited when manifesting magic, aligning each oval nub precisely into parallel lines running up his chest. The garment was tight enough to force his already deliberate posture even more erect, lending a stiffness to his movements. It was as uncomfortable as it was impractical, a current fashion of the wasted nobility who considered themselves the rulers of the Ceringion Reginum—a lofty self-evaluation that was less accurate than an initiate's first incantation, and doubly annoying.

He frowned at the stupidity of it all, bringing his thin brows sharply together. In truth, it mattered little what the vapid peerage selected for their method of communicating wealth to those around them, but he was cursed by the need to project a commensurate appearance. Under no circumstances would he be lumped together with those old grey mages who muttered over tomes in darkened rooms, plotting the fates of empires from the shadows while dressing in the same robes their great-grandfathers had worn. He was of the enlightened, those who sought a more public role for practitioners of sorcery in the affairs of the world, and with visibility came the requirement to look the part.

A display of precious metals about his fingers and ears would have completed the effect, but today he eschewed any jewelry, preferring to let the fine cut of his clothing say what needed to be said. None of the ensorcellments layered upon his rings would be of sufficient magnitude to influence the upcoming encounter anyway. He moved before a mirror and ran a hand over his shaven scalp, then smoothed the dark hairs of his tapered goatee.

Satisfied with his appearance, he exited his rooms. The suite—a coveted private space composed of a small study and even smaller bedchamber—was one of eight such arrangements occupying the eleventh floor of the Red Tower, so named for the hue of its granite walls and the myths of its origins as a center of punishment. He sealed the door closed with a mental command and a practiced flick of his fingers. The barrier, like every other within the tower, had no physical lock. Such paltry defenses would be useless against any of the practitioners who lived and worked here. Not that he held any concerns about those around him; locking the door was simply an automatic ritual.

Thick rugs muffled his footsteps as he traversed the hall and descended the gently curving sweep of the stairs circling the outer circumference of the tower. Tall windows of stained glass allowed sunlight to brighten the polished stone of the walls, and the glimpses of the outside provided vignettes of the other five towers of Solor-Majalis, the stronghold of the Conclave of Imaretii and one of the greatest centers of learning in the known world. Each of the six spires was the size of a city block at its base and joined to its neighbors in a hexagonal pattern by rectangular, balconied buildings seven stories high. It would have saved considerable effort to use some manner of magical conveyance to travel between destinations, but the ability to move oneself through space was one of the lost arts, not seen since the fall of the final Great Empire.

Today he was bound for the Grandmaster's tower, an added inconvenience as it could be entered only from the lowest levels. Still, any summons to that tower was exceedingly rare, and for such an invitation he was willing to endure the monotony of climbing stairs without complaint. Why he had been invited remained a mystery. The most plausible explanation was to discuss his upcoming examination to become a summoner, which, if he achieved it, would open doors into the upper echelons of the Conclave and give him command of a demon. Few within the Conclave had the talent to achieve such heights and fewer still were allowed it, no matter their talent. It had taken him almost two decades to master and demonstrate the needed skills, faster by years than most who attained the rank. He would make no assumptions, however. Within these walls, the obvious answer was often the most incorrect.

Felzig climbed to the eighteenth floor of the tower, reaching it at precisely the appointed time. Rather than the expected hallway bisecting the level, here he found only a small porch with double doors of dark wood, each inlaid with intricate golden patterns. He knocked once, unwilling to enter without permission.

"Come."

The thick, pleasant scent of ancient leather and wood greeted him as he stepped inside a chamber so vast as to seem impossible to fit within the confines of the tower walls. Deep, richly stained wooden shelves lined the room's circumference, rising towards the domed and muralled ceiling in a series of three tiers, each accessible via tightly spiraling staircases of dark metal. Their stoic solidness was broken only by six tall, peaked windows which stretched halfway up the walls. Thickly padded chairs were tucked into nooks beneath the windows, the perfect places to peruse one of the countless books overflowing every available shelf. A horned skull of impossible size dangled from the ceiling on thick iron chains, its pitted white surface awash in beams of light streaming from arrangements of glowing crystals high above. The collection of knowledge surrounding him would rival any in the civilized world, but its vast wealth was not what caught him off guard.

Felzig closed the door gently behind him, using the motion to mask his surprise at the two men who stood waiting for him beside a circular table in the center of the room: Fellaxus, Grandmaster of the Conclave; and Verelli, the most powerful of all those who answered to him. A private audience with Fellaxus was a great honor, just as one with Verelli was certain to be fraught with danger. This was clearly about more than just summoning.

Felzig evaluated each man as he approached. Had he passed them on the streets, he might have assumed the Grandmaster a beggar with his long grey beard and nondescript robes. Verelli's robes were also of the old style, though the cut and quality at least befitted his station. He was marred by a somewhat blocky head and the thick features of a commoner, however. At least he kept his chin cleanly shaved.

Both men's expressions were serious but not angry. Neither

man sat, a sign that Felzig's place here had not yet been earned, and so he clasped his hands behind his back and made no move towards the nearby chairs.

"We shall not waste your time with pleasantries," Fellaxus said, his words clipped and precise but not impatient. "There is a task of some delicacy that needs doing, and Master Verelli feels you will be the most capable person to complete it."

That was interesting. Verelli was the Grandmaster's de facto proxy, a prestigious position he unfortunately wasted by espousing views that were backwards and overly cautious. Worse, his disciples had been less than enthusiastic in their evaluations of Felzig's past performance. It was a perpetuation of the rot eating away at the Conclave's authority.

"I'm flattered, thank you," Felzig replied with the proper tones of respect. "What task?"

It was Verelli who answered. "At the risk of sounding dramatic, one that is critical to our survival. It will take you far away from here."

"How long, may I ask?"

"Three months, if you are sufficiently skilled."

Which, clearly, you hope that I am not.

"Further information will be supplied only if you commit yourself," Verelli continued. "Should you decline, you may return to your duties now."

Felzig could not tell whether Verelli hoped he would stay or go, but it was almost unheard of for someone of his level to be offered an opportunity like this, and so he was willing to take the gamble.

"If the Conclave believes it a worthy endeavor, I would be

honored to assist." *Now, let us see if the honor is worth it.*

Fellaxus exchanged an expressionless glance with Verelli, then motioned for him to begin.

"You are familiar with the various pantheons of the gods common in this region?" Verelli asked.

Felzig chafed at the obviousness of the answer. Verelli was always testing people. "As much as any of us who do not worship them. There are eight major and more than twenty minor deities represented on this continent. I can enumerate them, should you consider it helpful."

Verelli dismissed the offer. "Recent actions by two of the religious orders threaten to destabilize the equilibrium of the world and return us to the path that led to the downfall of the Three Great Empires."

It was, indeed, a cataclysmic prediction, one that was often used as justification for any number of actions by kings and sorcerers alike. It was likely an overreaction, but he was curious to know more.

"I haven't heard of any impending disaster," Felzig said.

"We would be disappointed if you had. These efforts are nascent and apparently coincidental, each centering on relics holy to their respective orders, but the sooner they are dealt with the less likely that events will get out of hand. The first is straightforward to handle and not a cause for concern. The more troubling, and delicate, situation involves the church of Amalthee."

Amalthee, goddess of wealth and knowledge. That piece of information could place this task in Ceringion or the neighboring Actondel, but the timeframe was long enough to allow him to make it anywhere within either kingdom. Felzig had traveled to many of Amalthee's churches in Actondel years ago and found that their clerics were well respected, at least for their scholarship. He waited for Verelli to continue rather than asking an incorrect question based on so little information.

"You have spent extensive time in the libraries of Amalthee, yes?" Verelli asked.

"As have we all. There are few places that can rival the compilation of great works they contain."

"It is true, and they are a boon to our work. The cause for concern revolves around a priest who now travels towards Actondel to take up the mantle of Legitarso—a reader of their sacred book."

Felzig was familiar with the myth of the Book of Amalthee. He had never been allowed to see it, of course, but had visited the church in Kirchmont, where it was said to be housed, numerous times. It began to make sense why they had chosen him. "If the legends are true and someone emerges who can unlock the secrets of that book, how would that affect us?"

"On the surface, it might appear beneficial," Verelli said. "It has been hundreds of years since any have been able to decipher that illustrious tone, and, if legend is to be believed, the secrets contained within could advance our understanding of magic by orders of magnitude. And therein lies the problem. How familiar are you with the fall of the last Great Empire?"

Felzig struggled to keep his annoyance at the barrage of historical questions in check. "Their hubris and wanton disregard for the safety of the practice of magic led to their downfall."

Verelli nodded. "Once united with the priest, we suspect that the Book will return to the holy city of Rappastall. The pontiff there has made no secret of his desire to share even the most secret knowledge with the entire population. The kingdoms surrounding the Mardrian Sea are fractured, many held together more by convenience than strength, but they remain in a period of general peace. We fear that unchecked use of magic will trigger a new wave of conquest, driving society to another even deeper collapse."

"This," Fellaxus said, finally joining the conversation, "is where your efforts will be focused. You are to delay, for a substantial period, the reuniting of reader and book."

"If the threat is so great, why not simply do away with this priest?" Felzig asked, instantly regretting the suggestion.

Verelli's eyes narrowed and his voice turned cold. "We do not wish untoward harm upon those we work so closely with, nor can we afford to draw undue attention to ourselves."

Felzig inclined his head in apology. "It was a purely mathematical observation of sacrifice versus reward, nothing more. The artifact resides in Kirchmont still?"

Verelli softened his stance, though only slightly. "By last reports. It is our understanding that you have been there before and have established a rapport with the priests?"

"Yes." He had also committed a journal detailing those visits to the library here, a reporting that clearly neither of these men had bothered to read.

"Iferion is already there and working towards a complementary goal. Seek him out only cautiously once your task is complete. Your collusion must not be discovered. Timing is critical. The priest has already arrived here in the Reginum and now follows the Gold Road west. Why he chose that direction remains a mystery, but it should allow you ample time to reach Kirchmont before he does. Captain Joloff will escort you there, along with an appropriate complement of retainers. He was born near the city and is familiar with the area and its inhabitants."

"I will be ready to leave as soon as he is," Felzig said, eager to end this conversation now that he understood what was being asked.

Verelli nodded. "There is one final detail: a junior mage will accompany you."

"An apprentice?" Felzig asked, this time unable to mask his surprise. A student was an unnecessary burden that he had long avoided, and this seemed a poor time to take one on.

"He has reached a level necessitating a more worldly view, and it will provide a convenient and completely valid reason for your journey to Kirchmont."

Curse Verelli for springing this on him, and in front of the grandmaster no less. "Who, if I may ask?"

"Honarch," Verelli answered. "He will introduce himself at your rooms in one hour."

Felzig recognized the name, that of a young mage whose star was rising faster than most. Talent did not always equate to ability, however. "How much of this does he know?"

"How much should he know?" Verelli asked. "The amount of information you choose to reveal will be left to your discretion, but he is a member of this Conclave and should not be misled. He, too, will be evaluated through this endeavor. However, you may wish to exercise caution with the more intimate details of what must be done."

Felzig cursed silently. Verelli made everything an evaluation. "I had hoped to delay taking on an apprentice until after completing my advancement to summoner. The effort required is considerable, as I'm certain you are aware, and I worry that the distraction will delay my testing. I would not want to disappoint anyone by falling behind."

A flicker of annoyance flashed across Verelli's features. "I can assure you that everything will be waiting for you upon your return, and you will retain your position. Should you feel the need to sooth your worries, speak to Orvonius before you leave and tell him you have my allowance to requisition your summoning focus now."

"You are most gracious, thank you," Felzig said, not meaning a word of it. "I shall see this task done."

He bowed politely, but when neither of the other two men returned the gesture, Felzig turned stiffly on his heel and left the room. Prestigious assignment or not, he would never forget the lack of courtesy. His retribution for their demeaning superiority was a thing for another time, however. Being so far removed from Solor-Majalis would limit his influence on events. Other wizards would surely seize the opportunity provided by his absence to advance their own position, no matter what promises Verelli made. The only lever he possessed would be to shorten the time he was gone, and that ran counter to the intention of a lengthy delay.

His mood continued to sour as he descended the stairs towards his next destination: one of the many shops arranged in a long gallery on the second floor of the Grandmaster's tower.

The busy public hall was not unlike any of the countless market streets that could be found in the wealthier parts of the city below, except that the vendors here were carefully vetted and more subdued in their efforts to draw attention to the clothing, delicacies, and other wares they had to offer. And it was reserved for a far more exclusive clientele. Orvonius' shop was tucked away along the outside wall, a surprisingly public place for such delicate and secretive work. The top of the door tapped against a small bell as Felzig entered the cramped space, and his nose was assaulted by the smells of metal and magic permeating the air. Gems, crystals, rings, and necklaces of every style imaginable were displayed artfully around the room, each catching the light streaming through a pair of large windows along the outer wall and reflecting it back in a dazzling kaleidoscope of color.

The jeweler sat hunched over his workbench, his fingers dancing in the air as they manipulated tiny spheres of light that heated and shaped the metal with a precision unmatched by even the finest mechanical implement. Orvonius was a bookish, unassuming man with a softness to his mannerisms that spoke to a life free of hardship. His was a singular talent for melding rare metals and equally scarce gemstones into works that were both beautiful and, for a select few, functional. He looked up over his jeweler's glasses at Felzig and chuckled.

"Verelli knew you'd be visiting. Said he was certain you would never accept his assurance alone."

Felzig longed to wipe the smirk from Orvonius' face, but he kept his reply neutral. "There is a reason Master Verelli occupies the position that he does, and I have no doubts as to the validity of his word."

Verelli and Orvonius could both rot in the hells for all he cared. Their games were petty, likely because neither were summoners themselves. The jeweler's predicament could at least be understood, as allowing him a demon would violate the directive separating the practitioners from those whose devices enabled the conjuring. Verelli's disability was reputed to be by choice, but Felzig suspected it was simply an area in which the man was not capable of succeeding. Why he would still be allowed such a high position when literally everyone even close to his level could summon remained a mystery.

Orvonius rose from his stool and turned towards the wall of small drawers behind him. "Well, that's between him and you, anyway." Producing a key from an inner pocket, he inserted it into a keyhole and turned it back and forth in a seemingly random but assuredly deliberate sequence. The surge of magic that accompanied the physical release of the lock was almost palpable, and far more powerful than he had expected.

Orvonius withdrew a small velvet pouch from within the tiny drawer. "It will be good for you to carry this around a while anyway," he said. "Helps with the attunement."

He produced a soft cloth edged in gold thread and laid it on a sunlit end of the counter, then pulled a single gemstone from the otherwise empty pouch and aligned it precisely in the middle. The deep green, slightly translucent stone was half the length of Felzig's smallest finger but not quite as large around, with dark veins that seemed to drift across its surface if he looked at it long enough. The cut was facetted but almost rectangular, with ends that came to sharp points.

"There's no setting?" Felzig asked.

"Not until the final binding. Just don't lose it between now and then."

"I'll be cautious," he promised, secreting it away inside a hidden fold behind the buttons of his robes. There was little allowance for pockets or pouches in garments so snug, but the discomfort of it poking into his chest was simply a reminder that it was there.

Orvonius returned to his seat. "Find me when you get back and we'll talk about that setting. And about how much it will cost."

Felzig scowled, but Orvonius' attention had already returned to his work. He left the jeweler without another word and made his way back towards his own tower, his mood darkening with every step.

The prestige of having the focus was a hollow victory without the demon's name to go with it. Those were far more difficult to come by, and he, like everyone else not directly involved in their procurement, had no idea how they were discovered. The manner in which they would be allocated was better understood. The strength of each demon was carefully matched against the wizard who was to receive it, and so he expected an exceptional demon to align with his abilities. He was already aware of the mage who would follow him—a weaker, less capable sorceress—and she would not hesitate to preempt his claim during his absence. There was only one way to ensure that such a theft never happened, but it was a dangerous gamble. The solution struck him suddenly, and before he could debate the wisdom of what he was about to do, he had already altered course. Rather than ascending the outer stairs towards his room, he turned down a narrow hallway which led him to an interior stairwell that descended into a gloomy darkness.

The next hallway he reached was far narrower than the ones above and largely empty of people. He had purpose in this part of the citadel only rarely but often enough that no one he passed questioned his being there.

There was no inviting entryway here, only a heavy door of solid oak with bands of iron to block the way. His fear of being caught standing there overrode the doubt that caused him to hesitate, and he knocked softly.

After what felt like an eternity, the peephole snapped open, and a woman peered out at him through the narrow slit. She closed the peephole just as quickly, threw the bolt with a loud clang, and opened the door.

"Why are you here?" she asked without fanfare.

"Master Calista, so good to see you again," he said, entering the room as quickly as he dared without appearing suspicious.

Calista was a stern woman who looked older than she probably was. There was nothing about her that would be considered attractive, save for her abundant bosom. It seemed a useless bulk to carry around, something that would impede normal activity, and he was thankful that he did not have to suffer such needless weight on his own personage.

"What do you want?" she asked, plopping down unhappily in a threadbare chair whose upholstery had probably begun to unravel before either of them was born.

"You're particularly cheerful today. Has it been too long since they let you up to see the sun?"

"Sunlight affects my work poorly," she said with a dramatic sigh.

Having both reached the limits of their ability to banter, Felzig settled down to business.

"I was told that I could receive my name early."

Calista instantly became guarded. "I was not informed of that."

"That doesn't surprise me. I literally just came from a meeting with Masters Verelli and Fellaxus."

"*You* met with Master Fellaxus?"

Felzig nodded smugly. "There is something I've been asked to do, something that will take me away for some time and potentially delay my advancement. As an accommodation, I have been allowed to obtain one component of the process."

It was the truth, just not all of it.

"A very generous offer," she said.

"Indeed. It seemed improper, but I did not wish to offend him by refusing."

Her foot began to tap nervously.

"It will remain sealed," Felzig assured her. "It's not as if it will do me any good until the final binding."

"True. And it's all but useless without the focus. Well, Verelli can make those decisions." Her eyes narrowed. "And you swear not to break the seal?"

"On my life," Felzig said, meaning it. "You know I'm a stickler for details."

"Alright. Wait here."

She rose and disappeared into the back room. Felzig waited anxiously, hoping that no one else would come to disturb them. He had reached a point where there would be no way to deny what he was doing, should he be discovered.

Calista returned a few moments later carrying only a plain envelope. Felzig feared that she had changed her mind until she thrust the folded paper towards him.

"The seal is to be broken only in the presence of your instructor during the final examination. Do so before then at your own peril."

Felzig turned the envelope over and saw that it was held fast with black sealing wax that bore the summoner's vortex symbol.

"Understood," he said, hiding the envelope away with the summoning focus. "I was advised not to speak of this to anyone other than you, lest some of the other candidates become jealous and try to talk you into doing the same."

Calista rolled her eyes. "That's all I need: a bunch of unqualified summoners demanding their names early. No one will hear of this from my lips, and I trust it won't be shared from yours either."

She shooed him out of the room, almost as eager to be rid of him as he was to leave, and locked the door behind him.

Felzig forced his pace to remain unhurried as he ascended back to the above-ground levels, but he did not breathe easily until he was safely back in his rooms. There would be repercussions should anyone find out what he had done, but they could be smoothed over, and everything would proceed as it should. His place was assured, and the demon he was meant to have would still be his. Now it was time to gather his things and see to this new apprentice.

* * *

The knock on Felzig's door came precisely at the appointed hour but far sooner than he would have preferred. He closed the chest he had been loading and took a quick inventory of the room to make sure that nothing sensitive was visible.

"Enter," he commanded.

The door opened, and Honarch stepped into the room. The younger man was dressed in a deep red, a color that complimented the reddish tinge of his short beard. His hair, in alignment with the current fashion, was relatively short, not quite reaching his shoulders but slightly disheveled as if it was a child intent on misbehaving. His robes were the newer style that many of the young wizards had adopted, loosely wrapped about the top and belted snugly at the waist. The sleeves were long, much like the robes of old, but the hem short, falling only to the knee with splits down the sides to allow movement. Grey pants with boots that came halfway up his shins completed the look. It was an interesting assortment, but one which Felzig generally agreed with. There might be some hope for this relationship yet.

"Master Felzig," Honarch said with an appropriately proper dip of his head. "It is a pleasure to meet you in person."

"We will see if that sentiment still holds at the end of this conversation," Felzig said, waving him to a chair. He had never been one to waste time with idle chatter when there was work to be done, and he saw no reason to delay matters now. Still, he had to be careful about how much he revealed. "Are you aware of why you have been assigned as my apprentice?"

"Not in specifics," Honarch replied, taking a seat. "But I'm certain that you have much to teach."

Teaching was the last thing Felzig wanted to be burdened with, but he would do what he must. "I have been selected by the Grandmaster for a mission of utmost importance, one that coincides with your need to see more of the world. For this purpose, we have been paired together."

"That seems agreeable."

There was excitement in his response, but Felzig considered the lack of challenge from the young man to mean he was either too naive or too trusting for his own good. Or perhaps he was already aware of more than he was letting on. Honarch should have been suspicious about such a proclamation, but whatever his thoughts, he held any questions that he might have had.

"We'll be traveling to Actondel," Felzig said, "leaving in the morning. I will convey more of what we are about as it becomes necessary, but for now you may know that you will be evaluated throughout this entire endeavor. We will be surrounded by those who are not proficient in the ways of magic and cannot be trusted with its secrets, and who will likely place us in peril. Thus, some degree of discretion will be in order."

"The Conclave does need to be more active in Actonel," Honarch said eagerly. "Their nation exchanges so many ideas with ours, and it seems a wonderful opportunity to display our talents in a more positive light."

Felzig stroked his dark goatee and frowned at his apprentice's answer. The right words were there, but he did not entirely trust the man's intentions. It was time to push the issue and see where his thoughts leaned.

"That is incorrect," he said. "Our purpose with magic is not to 'better the world' or 'make people happy.' What is most important is for us to maintain our position of power and guide events along the course they must take."

Honarch frowned. "But people will eventually notice that they are being controlled. How does that help?"

Felzig smiled in a way that was not in the least about pleasure. "That is where the style, the art, the craft of being a member of the Conclave comes into play." He began to pace slowly as he talked. "We, the most knowledgeable people in this realm, know best what to do. This is accomplished through rigorous study and research, not through concern for emotional frailty. By examining the mistakes of the past, we can prevent the calamities of the future. That stewardship cannot be done from a position of weakness."

Honarch glanced out the window in the direction of the harbor. "But would encouraging cooperation not be a gentler road to the same ends? Take a ship's crew, for example. Combined they—"

"—are nothing without their captain," Felzig finished for him. "Let us consider those ships you mention. Each one is organized, financed, and commanded by someone in authority; their tasks are appointed not by the crew but by those who own them. Say that one of these ships sets out into the sea, and three days from shore the captain falls ill and perishes along with all the senior officers. What would happen?"

"The crew would continue to sail the ship."

"Would they do so harmoniously? Do you think they would band together and work as one for the common good, or would you expect some to use the lack of authority as an excuse to further their own ends? The vacuum of power lends weight to each man's own self-interest."

"They would not do anything to jeopardize the ship or their own survival," Honarch protested.

"Ah, but wouldn't they? Do you truly believe that the entire crew would continue to work, even with no one there to tell them what to do and when to do it? Some would toil diligently doing the tasks they must, knowing it was for the good of all. Still others would become lazy and do nothing. No, a new captain would arise, whether through consensus or conquest."

"But a nation is not a ship," Honarch countered, "and inherently more resilient due to its size."

"What is a ship but a tiny nation? Do you suppose that a larger version would continue to function any more successfully without a leader?"

Honarch's brow furrowed as he considered. "They would struggle in the same way, but, to your point, leaders will always emerge, if not from the nobility then from the temples."

"The temples are weak." Felzig smashed a fist into his palm to emphasize the point, frustrated at talking in circles. "Their knowledge is passive, affecting nothing. Take the followers of Toush. They wander everywhere, making people happy. And what good does it do in the end? When they've gone, what becomes of their charity? It is squandered on those who don't know enough to use it." Ready to be done with the conversation, he waved aside any reply before it could be uttered. "There will be ample time to debate these philosophies as we travel. Return to me at sunrise prepared to leave."

Annoyance flashed across Honarch's face at the sudden dismissal, but he rose and bowed with enough politeness that Felzig did not chastise him for the silent insolence. "I shall be prepared."

He made no response as the younger wizard left, certain that this apprentice was simply an anchor meant to slow him down. At least he would be able to count on Iferion to do things that needed to be done. He, at least, was no ally of Verelli's, and his thoughts tended to flow the same way as Felzig's did. It seemed no mere coincidence that two of Verelli's opponents were being sent away, but there was no escaping it now.

He returned to preparing for the journey, a process that occupied him well into the night. When he was at last finished selecting, cataloging, and stowing his clothing, books, and effects, he sat, exhausted from the day. His body required sleep, but his mind wandered instead to the victory he had secured. After a whispered command to ensure the door was locked, he pulled the envelope from his pocket.

He turned it over several times, analyzing every minute detail of the paper. It was amazing how much power could be conveyed by the simple arrangement of fibers and ink now held in his hand. The soft wax of the seal was warm and pliable beneath his fingertips, but he made no move to break it. There was no need. By its simple possession he had everything he required.

Felzig smiled to himself before putting it away, already anticipating the day when he would discover which demon's name was written within.

Perhaps no character in the *Guardian's Prophecy* series rose to prominence as unexpectedly as the demon Mataasrhu. Even I was unaware of just how deeply entwined in our heroes' lives he would become when he made his first appearance at the beginning of *Weaponforger*. That his path and Tormjere's were destined to cross was no more than a timely coincidence, but as Tormjere once pointed out, coincidence can often reveal a greater truth.

Of all the cities, kingdoms, and fantastical locations of this world that we travelled through, none have surpassed the demonic realm of Urtratu with the sheer number of requests to further explore it. There is something incredibly fascinating about that place, with its hellish landscape and harsh conditions, and a way of life so impossibly far from our own. It is a bleak world of conflict and death, diametrically opposed to the existence of anyone or anything not born there, yet it was always a place that our heroes were destined to venture.

But not without a guide.

And, perhaps, not without a friend.

The influence of Mataasrhu's participation was felt long before his name was made known, but his destiny, like Tormjere's, was never entirely his own…

Edict of Servitude

"Mataasrhu!"

The echoes of the summons raced the length of the cavern to invade the sanctity of his burrow. Though he was wedged tightly into the hollowed-out space, the solidness of the rock walls that surrounded him offered no protection from the verbal assault. Anger rumbled in Mataasrhu's throat, but there it stayed. One did not ignore the summons of an Attuned.

He uncoiled himself from within his protective enclosure as slowly as he dared. Rising to his full height, he planted his hooved feet squarely, tensing every muscle in his already sizable body. Those demons of his *wharra* who were near backed away, the more cautious of them turning their backs to him in submission. Their reactions validated his status as the most powerful among them all, save one, but he could not savor the moment. His attention was focused on the far end of the cavern where three demons awaited him beneath the curving maw of the entrance.

Most prominent was Zadrhu, the Attuned who had called him out. The tentacles that draped from his blackened scalp writhed with a vigor they rarely displayed. With him stood Norlrhu, a hulking demon with overlarge arms that had allowed him to bludgeon his way to the top. The lord of the wharra was the only demon within it that Mataasrhu could not best. Yet now, the fearsome leader's small wings drooped and his back was turned towards the final demon standing with them: an Attuned that Mataasrhu did not recognize. This newcomer was ancient, with deeply textured skin weathered like sandblasted rocks as old as the canyon outside. The tentacles growing from his skeletally thin head were so great in number that their weight pulled him forward into a hunch, but to mistake his stature for weakness would be fatal.

It was towards them that Mataasrhu walked, the evil jeers and derisive hoots of his wharra following his every step. The grunts and shrieks emanating from the long faces of the grey-furred *hadraal* were the loudest, but this was unsurprising, given his past conflicts with them. They were beasts who would never achieve his level of dominance and, like all creatures who could not hope to be as worthy, they hated him for it. Mataasrhu strode through them as if it were he who had arranged this spectacle. He would not crawl like some craven Nameless one.

Reaching the trio, Mataasrhu turned his back respectfully to the pair of Attuneds, a motion that left him squarely facing Norlrhu. The leader of the wharra bared his teeth at the insult, but his answering challenge was preempted by their visitor.

"This one shall be taken under the Edict," the ancient Attuned rasped.

"Our Mistress has spoken," Zadrhu echoed.

Mataasrhu had no idea what they were talking about, nor did he care for the implication that anything would happen against his will. Norlrhu's smug triumph was so grating that he almost challenged the leader right there, regardless of the Attuneds' wishes.

The ancient one extended an arm, pushing Mataasrhu with surprising force towards the exit. Mataasrhu obeyed as he had to, though his skin crawled at being touched in such a manner. Were anyone else in the cave to do so, he would have torn them apart and reclaimed them on the spot. Even worse than being shoved about, he was left wondering what this aimless talking was for. Norlrhu was clearly pleased at this turn of events, which meant nothing good for Mataasrhu.

He was determined to show neither hesitation nor fear to the ancient Attuned as they traversed the short curve of the tunnel. There was no knowing what lurked in the openness of the canyon beyond, but he prepared himself for whatever trial might await. Yet even with such forethought, he was taken aback by the might of the demon awaiting him.

An angular head dominated by rows of sharp teeth gazed down on him from far above with cruel calculation. The breadth of Mataasrhu's own shoulders could not match the narrowest part of this demon's leg, and just one of the cloven hooves could have ground him to nothing. The dark, powerful reds of the demon's skin were crossed by the scars of a thousand battles and marred by patches of mottled black, testament to the hellish fires which had failed to defeat him.

The demon raised himself to his full height and stretched his wings wide, blotting out the sky.

"*This* is what you have found?" he demanded, as Mataasrhu quickly turned his back. "I would question if this puny thing has even been named."

Mataasrhu's anger at the insult threatened to override his sense of self-preservation.

"He is the correct size for what must be done, Sulfaxrhu," the Attuned said. "And notice his control."

Sulfaxrhu bent down until his massive head was even with Mataasrhu's. "That is because he knows what will be done to him should he choose otherwise. Make certain then, and let us be on our way before the dirt of this place contaminates me further."

Mataasrhu risked a sideways glance at the Attuned, bracing himself against the pain of whatever ritual magic was about to befall him.

The Attuned ignored him, turning his gaze instead towards the impenetrable clouds far above, reading the will of their goddess within the tumultuously dark swirls. "His servitude is ordained," the Attuned stated. "As our mistress commands, so shall we follow."

Sulfaxrhu's lip curled in disgust. "Come then, little beast. Prepare yourself to serve."

Mataasrhu had no idea what that meant, but comparing him to the furry animals who existed far beneath his own status was incendiary and it was all he could do to resist demanding an explanation.

The Attuned's tentacles flailed about as he muttered some incantation. Mataasrhu felt the air around his legs become firm, taking on substance as dense as the rock beneath his hooves yet as pliable as the flesh of a vanquished enemy. It was an unnatural, revolting sensation that set his teeth on edge. His body rebelled at the loss of control, certain that his life was now at risk. Aware of Sulfaxrhu's contemptuous stare, however, he forced himself to give no reaction as he began to float upwards.

The ancient Attuned rose with him, their rate of ascent steadily increasing the higher they went. Sulfaxrhu soared through the air in sweeping spirals around them. Mataasrhu longed to have wings such as those. To attain such heights without them would have meant climbing the craggy walls of the canyon, an act that would spell certain death, should he have ventured here alone. Neither of the demons with him held similar fears—the denizens of these levels kept themselves far from the attentions of such might.

A blast of wind struck Mataasrhu as they broke free of the canyon rim, and he was thrust into a realm he had never known existed. Vast plains of sand so deeply orange that they were almost brown stretched in every direction. In the distance, mountains rose, sharp, jagged peaks of striated browns and ochres.

It was unnatural to behold the entirety of the clouded sky from one horizon to the other, appearing as if the world of the canyons he had occupied his entire life had been inverted. And above it all boiled the dark, ever-swirling clouds of the *Nerravor*. He had only seen glimpses of Mergolatrhu's Shroud through the slit ceiling of the canyon, but to witness the full magnitude of its power was incomprehensible.

The abrasiveness of the blowing sand scoured his skin as he and the Attuned returned to the ground, coming to rest where the smooth plains met the columns and crags of rock marking the canyon's edge. The soft material beneath his hooves gave way slightly with each step, a novel and disconcerting sensation.

Without the comforting walls of the canyon to put at his back, Mataasrhu felt naked and vulnerable in such an open expanse. He tried, but he could not resist the urge to constantly look over his shoulder.

"None shall harm you while you cower in my shadow, little one," Sulfaxrhu sneered as he landed with an earth-shaking crunch.

It was not Mataasrhu's place to question that proclamation, but his ire escaped before he could stop it. "Do I have your bargain?" he snapped.

The ground slammed into him from below, and his vision danced as it turned to smears of reds and browns. He tried to twist away from the sudden pain stabbing through his body but could not. As his vision returned, he saw that he was flat on his back, impaled by the talons on Sulfaxrhu's hand. Sulfaxrhu's head bent towards his own, ready to end him in one bite.

"Do not presume that you are worthy of my obligations," the greater demon hissed.

The pain was blinding, but Mataasrhu clamped his mouth shut and ignored the dark blood leaking from his body, refusing to give Sulfaxrhu the sign of weakness that he wanted.

"We should proceed," the Attuned interrupted. "I shall hasten him along."

"He can walk, like all the others," Sulfaxrhu countered as he withdrew.

"I have not asked for favors," Mataasrhu said, forcing himself to his hooves. His leg barely held his weight, yet he would willingly end himself before admitting to any weakness.

Sulfaxrhu smirked but seemed to approve of the display. "Then restore yourself, but be quick." His rumbling voice turned threatening once more. "Fall behind me, even by one step, and your life will end."

Mataasrhu cast about, searching the protruding rocks. He

found what he was looking for: a pile of weathered rock that was more black than red. It had been there for some time, clearly, but the vague outline suggested the form of a demon lying in the sand. He limped over to it and broke off a piece of what might have once been a shoulder. Who it had been was even less relevant than how he had died—just another of the countless casualties in the unending contest of superiority that defined their existence. Whoever it was had returned the substance from which he was made to the world, and Mataasrhu hoped only that his remnants were still potent.

He ground the soft black rock to dust in his hands, then pressed it against his wounds. The coarse powder congealed to a paste when mixed with his own dark blood, taking on the texture and consistency of his own flesh as it dried. Such intrinsic abilities were granted to all those of his race by Mergolatrhu, she who had created them from this world and given them dominion over the lesser animals living upon it.

Once made whole, Mataasrhu took his place ahead of Sulfaxrhu without hesitation, not bothering to test the strength of the repair. The greater demon pointed him in a direction, and then they were off.

Mataasrhu was forced into a fast jog to keep ahead of Sulfaxrhu's longer strides while the Attuned floated along at Sulfaxrhu's right hand, seemingly oblivious to them both. Out of spite or hurry, the winged demon pushed their pace ever faster, and Mataasrhu's chest heaved with the effort of maintaining his tenuous lead. Unwilling to consider what would happen should he stumble; he turned his concentration towards their apparent destination.

They were headed directly towards a distant but infinitely tall rock spire that could only be Golardrhu, that legendary pathway through the Nerravor upon which the mightiest demons would fight their way to the top. Most demons would live and die having never seen the brutal ritual known as the Rending Reclamation. Sulfaxrhu's might was the greatest Mataasrhu had ever beheld, however, an opinion validated by the fact that nothing was attacking them on the exposed plain. There were whispers that the ritual was imminent, so it could be Sulfaxrhu intended to initiate it himself.

"Turn towards that triple column," Sulfaxrhu commanded, dashing the idea.

Mataasrhu obeyed instantly, altering course towards a closer cliff edge where three curved fingers of rock jutted above the rim. He was nearing the limits of his endurance when they at last reached the lip of that other much broader chasm. A wide path dropped below the rim and their pace barely slowed as they turned onto it.

The track descended only a short distance into the canyon before arriving at the entrance to a cave unlike any he had ever beheld. Where the tunnels he was familiar with were narrow and twisting to enhance their defensibility, this one was frighteningly wide and straight. All three of them could have walked into it shoulder to shoulder—if it had been allowed—and still have had room on either side, and it was so tall that even Sulfaxrhu would need use of his wings to reach the ceiling. Heat emanated from within, radiating into the open air in a wasteful display of superiority.

The Attuned settled to the ground beside them. "We are

expected," he said with confidence, though the faintest tremor marred his statement.

Sulfaxrhu, wings tucked tight against his back, regarded the portal warily before motioning Mataasrhu forward.

Mataasrhu obeyed reluctantly, aware of the higher pitch of his own small hooves next to the steady thump of Sulfaxrhu's. The tunnel entered the canyon wall at a slant and made only the slightest turn at the end, a design that seemed more for privacy than for defense.

Dozens of burning barrels encircled the cavern, their flickering light providing sufficient illumination that there was no need to call upon his innate ability to see in the dark. In the center of the expanse rested an immense creature, one matching the legends of the monsters who roamed the depths of the lower canyons.

Mataasrhu spun away before eye contact could be made, cowering so abjectly that it left him curled into a ball on the floor.

"*This* is what you have found?" The voice was deep, like the moaning of the canyons during a storm, and it rolled and crashed through the enclosed space with such fury that Mataasrhu felt the vibrations in his bones.

"She wills it to be thus," the Attuned said.

"He shows potential for what must be done, mighty Zrahzaxrhu," Sulfaxrhu said.

Mataasrhu barely heard them. His only concern now was finding some way to emerge from this cave alive, a goal that seemed less likely with every passing moment.

The cavern shook with thunderous footsteps as the colossus named Zrahzaxrhu closed on them. "I find that doubtful. The consequences of his failure could undo all."

Mataasrhu dared not risk a glance at any of them, certain that even the slightest movement would earn him his death.

The Attuned was more resilient in standing his ground, yet even his voice quivered as he spoke. "The lesser animals have proven unsuited to the task, lacking the intellect for anything beyond brute force. They are also more likely to violate the silence, which is why we muzzle them as they are sent to the otherworld of Harlairdra."

Mataasrhu did not know why, but the twisted nature of that name filled him with revulsion even as the concept of a world other than his own pulled at his curiosity.

"Speak to him of the prophecy," Zrahzaxrhu commanded, making some gesture that buffeted him with wind, "so that he might understand how he is to obey."

"Listen then, little one," the Attuned said.

Mataasrhu turned his eyes towards the Attuned as respect demanded, thankful to be given a safe way to direct his attention.

The ancient one lifted his head up as though seeking the clouds that raged somewhere above the ceiling of rock. "Our Mistress of Torments, Mergolatrhu, makes her will known to us through the messages of the clouds. She has spoken and told us this: a pretender god of another world comes again to destroy our own. We name this false god Loyarhu and speak of her in contempt."

Loyarhu. The Light Stealer. The being said to have plunged the world into darkness and stolen its bounty. Mataasrhu had heard Zadrhu speak of such things, but that mythical being was a distant concept beyond its insidious influence on whatever battle was at hand.

"Long have we warred with this false god," the Attuned

continued, "and the time of our victory approaches. We must draw the Light Stealer into a war of our own choosing rather than of hers, and for that we must seek out her champion upon another world. This is the task to which you will be given."

"Does your small awareness comprehend what is at stake?" Zrahzaxrhu demanded.

Mataasrhu did not. This talk of other worlds and other gods left his head spinning, but to admit to ignorance would surely be fatal. "I understand, mighty Zrahzaxrhu."

The raw heat of the massive demon's breath burned his back as Zrahzaxrhu bent close, and Mataasrhu groveled so low that he wished he could tunnel into the ground like a rock eater.

"Take care that you do. Your death will mean nothing, but should you fail, should you spoil our coming victory, there will be no place on this world or any other where you may hide yourself from me."

Zrahzaxrhu straightened his massive bulk. "Ensure that he is made ready."

There was no telling who the command was addressed to, but it was Sulfaxrhu who kicked him to his feet and towards the exit.

Mataasrhu practically ran from the cave without looking back, his shoulders hunched and his head down. Only when he reached the ledge outside did he realize that the Attuned was the only one still with him.

The ancient demon gestured, seizing Mataasrhu about the waist with solidified air once more. Then they were flying.

Up and out of the canyon they streaked at unbelievable speeds, crossing windswept planes of sand and weaving between jagged mountains. Mataasrhu held himself rigid, though there was nothing else to be done within the grasp of the Attuned's magic. At last, they plummeted into the depths of another rocky crevasse, landing at the bottom before an alien structure.

It was a strange arrangement of flattened and equally sized blocks aligned atop identical rounded columns, all carved directly from the rock wall. The unnatural smoothness of the stone was foreboding, made all the more so by the impenetrable black rectangle of the entrance it surrounded. The fear twisting within Mataasrhu's belly escaped as an admission of weakness to himself.

"I do not understand."

The tentacles on the Attuned's head writhed in wicked anticipation as he seized Mataasrhu by the shoulder and flung him into the darkness. "Your education is just beginning."

Introduction to
"The Seventh Path"

The coming-of-age transformations that Eljorn and Tormjere endured were significantly different but equally abrupt. Their gifts, each a mixture of innate talent and divine intervention, manifested in equally incongruous ways. Tormjere's developing skills ultimately received the lion's share of attention, overshadowing those of his younger brother.

Which is ironic, because the latter half of this story was the first scene that I ever imagined, and also the first one ever committed to paper. I'm not entirely certain why it came to mind so readily, though it had the utmost relevance to the plot as originally envisioned. Perhaps it was a remnant of all the Bruce Lee and Chuck Norris movies I watched as a child, or maybe it sprang from every dreamer's desire to be uniquely different.

Whatever its source, the scene was fully imagined but only half complete when it was cut from *Eyes of the Blind*. That path was never walked—one of a million unrealized futures that might have been.

This part of Eljorn's story, like so many other tales that never made it into the finished manuscript, remains close to my heart, and it gives me no small amount of joy to finally share it with you.

The Seventh Path

Eljorn sat uncomfortably on the hard wooden floor, trying to focus. His eyes were closed and his breathing slow and deep, as it should be when meditating. His posture was equally proper, with crossed legs and a straight back, and with his hands resting on his knees. The peaceful sounds of the monastery complex filtered inside the training hall through the windows, their openness a concession to the heat of the late spring day. The gentle breeze that dried the sweat from the brows of the nearly forty white-robed dimnants seated around him brought with it the smell of flowers and the deep, soothing tones of the wooden chimes that hung from the corner of almost every building. It was as serene and contemplative a place as could be found, yet his thoughts remained unexpectedly turbulent.

There was really no reason they should be so unsettled. Since arriving here at the end of the Journey of Entry—that long walk that had carried him halfway across the Kingdom—the time studying and training had flown by, with days turning to weeks and weeks to months. Were it not for the changing of the seasons as they advanced from fall to winter and on into spring, he would have had no idea how long he had been there. Distance and degree were of far greater import than time to a follower of Toush. He and his fellow dimnants had been strengthened through countless lessons, both physical and mental, and they now stood ready to advance to the next phase of their training.

Or rather, sat ready. Which was half of his problem.

His physical location should not have made this particular exercise so challenging. His calling to the service of Toush, the Walker of Paths, had been no mistake. Becoming a monk had been everything he expected it to be, and in every facet of his studies he had excelled. All, that is, except for meditation. The calming state that had always come so naturally to him at home had proved vexingly difficult to achieve no matter how perfect the surroundings.

Today had been another long, grueling time of study and physical practice, one that had begun well before the sun rose. The inclusion of open-handed fighting techniques had been a mild surprise given the pacifistic reputation of the order, but it made sense given the amount of time they would one day spend alone as they followed their paths.

Some of the exercises had them doing their routines while balanced atop the shoulders of two other dimnants. At other times they maneuvered across poles and beams, struggling not to fall off as they completed their task. Discipline of the body was just as important as the mind, and he did find his thoughts clearer after such vigorous exercise. It seemed unlikely to solve his issues of concentration today, but Toush was a patient god. Eljorn was confident that He would show him the way in His own time.

Despite such certainty, he missed his home, he admitted, which was the other half of his problem. Spring was the time when he and Tormjere would climb to the overlook to admire the annual rebirth of the forest and dream of the future. Painfully real, an image of his brother standing alone on that ridge leapt into his mind. The sorrow in his brother's eyes was palpable, triggering a sudden surge of emotion that washed the image away as quickly as it had come.

That was odd, he thought, forcing his mind back to his immediate environment.

The timing gong sounded outside, marking the end of the session. Before the echoing tones had faded into silence, Eljorn was on his feet and headed towards the open doors with all the other students. To be slow was to be inattentive, and attention to detail was the only way to know if one was on the correct path.

Once outside, the group filed down the steps and crossed the flagstones of a large courtyard—the same one they used to practice their katas every morning, rain or shine—and continued between another pair of buildings towards their residence hall, an oblong structure tucked into a corner of the complex against the outer curtain wall. The movement was accomplished without the usual banter that groups of young men typically enjoyed, for every first-level dimnant was bound to remain mute for the initial phase of their training, a condition designed to increase their comfort with silence and seclusion. The relationship this fostered amongst the dimnants was one of loyalty and respect but not of friendship. At least, not yet. Eljorn considered it less a stripping away of their identity and more of a metamorphosis. What had come before their arrival was just one of the paths they would walk. Where their roads would take them in the future, only Toush knew.

Take, for example, this monastery. The walled complex devoted to the Walker of Paths was appropriately secluded in a hilly, forested region somewhere near the Wiermist Woods. The central temple was a squared structure of four levels stacked atop each other, each smaller than the one beneath it. Sharply sloping roofs overhung each level, their steep sides adept at shedding the heavy snows that fell here during the winter. The majority of the other buildings were only a single story, their floors raised from the ground to the height of Eljorn's head by solid stone footings. Broad rounded steps led up to the single entrance of each. Though he considered the design of this place to be pleasing, Eljorn could not keep himself from glancing longingly at the woods just beyond the wall.

Why do we have to sit in a dark room to think?

It was his only real complaint. The obvious answer, of course, was because this was what the instructors, respectfully referred to as Elder Uncles, expected of them. The directions he and all the other first-level dimnants operated under were clear: solitude was required, and talking was not allowed. They were to focus their thoughts on the tenants of Toush and receive such guidance as was revealed.

Paths.

The ability to identify, evaluate, and select the proper path from the options presented at any given time was a skill they practiced daily. Some choices were innocuous, altering one's course through life ever so slightly. Others were momentous, capable of influencing the paths of far more than oneself. He could, for example, choose to walk on the left or right side of the walkway, just as he could choose to retreat to his cell or not.

Could he?

They were expected to spend the remainder of the evening in solitary contemplation. The most intuitive location for that activity was in their cells, as that was where they would be fed and spend the rest of the night, but at no time had they been explicitly commanded to do so. That was a logical assumption based on the intent of the given directions, certainly, but an assumption it remained.

The residence hall loomed before him, with most of the dimnants ahead of him having already mounted the steps and entered the building. The time to choose was almost past.

Without breaking stride, Eljorn turned sharply to the right and stepped out of line, continuing at the same brisk pace towards the far end of the building. Furtive glances cast by the other dimnants were the only objection raised. Around the corner he found a small gate—unlocked, to his surprise—which allowed passage through the outer wall.

Passing through that barrier granted an unexpectedly strong sense of freedom, though the defensive measure was intended to keep the wild creatures of the woods out rather than hold the monks in, and he paused to examine the area.

The woods here appeared little different than those surrounding Kenzing, sloping uphill and becoming steeper the farther one traveled away from the monastery. In truth, he would have been content to sit just outside the gate with his back against the wall and stare at the trees. An inviting footpath wound its way off to his left, however, beckoning him onward. He followed the narrow track as it paralleled the outer wall for around half its length then turned away, rising steadily and cresting a hill before dropping sharply. A narrow creek cut across the trail here, and, while its flowing water was not even half as wide as that of his creek back home, Eljorn was overjoyed to have found it.

He removed his sandals before stepping off the trail and onto the rocks. It would have been deeply rewarding to continue clambering across the wet stones of the creek as it hooked away from the monastery, dropping down a steep incline towards a sheltered clearing before finally wandering out of sight, but he stopped three steps in, alighting atop a boulder which was both large and dry enough for his purposes. Settling cross-legged onto his chosen seat, he watched the waters tumble down the hill and across the trail towards him.

Eljorn closed his eyes and, for the first time since he had arrived, truly relaxed. The sounds of the flowing water brought with it a clarity that could only be achieved from a calm mind, validating his choice to come here. It was strange that such a small change in setting could produce so profound an effect, providing perspective on what had been troubling him. Through this lens, Kenzing became a starting point rather than a needed destination, an anchor to who and what he was. The past came into alignment with the present, both positioning him for what would come next.

It was in this relaxed, almost trance-like state that he remained. Time slipped away and the woods began to dim as the evening grew longer, until the deep crash of the timekeeping gong roused him from his deliberations. Eljorn could almost see the ripples of sound as they traveled across his closed eyes. It was gone before he could even react to the surprising vision, but any hope of studying it fled as his eyes opened and he jumped to his feet. It would be unacceptable to be late for the meal. Nevertheless, he was certain that his brief observation held some significance. What, exactly, that might be was something best left for another time. Every path began with the first step, and Eljorn could be as patient as he was persistent.

* * *

He returned to that spot in the creek every night for a week, cherishing those quiet times of peaceful reflection. His new daily habit had garnered him neither punishment nor reward, and while several of his fellow dimnants seemed envious of his explorations, not a one had followed him outside the walls.

But it was the visualization of the sound from the timing gong that intrigued him the most, its every use providing him with flickers of perception that were anything but normal. Such sensations struck him nowhere else within the compound, and yet nothing about the creek suggested any mystical empowerment. He could attribute it only to his state of mind.

It was as he sat in the creek exploring this dichotomy on one pleasant afternoon when the scuff of a foot on dirt interrupted his musings. Eljorn cracked one eye open, expecting to see one of the more adventuresome dimnants come to join him, or one of the instructors finally tired of his transgressions. Instead, he was greeted by a group of perhaps half a dozen men in common garb approaching rapidly. There was no telling who they might be or what they were about, but each carried a wooden staff or cudgel.

Eljorn forced himself to remain motionless, denying his instinct to jump into action like a startled deer. Silently repeating a calming mantra to himself, he evaluated the men through his slit eyelids as they drew closer. Their pace was purposeful, but the weapons they carried were held casually, and their attention was given more to their route than to him. The troop passed him by in silence before descending along the trail to the clearing below. The last figure in line, a man with almost-shaved hair and dressed in the worn-out red robes of a common monk, wandered along at a far less serious gait. The monk was a reassuring, if odd, addition to the group, but as none of them had paid Eljorn any mind, he would give them the same courtesy.

Once they were out of sight, he took a deep breath to center himself and closed his eyes once more. The timekeeping gong would be struck soon, and he needed to be ready for whatever feelings it evoked in him. A sensation did arrive moments later, but it came in the form of a puff of air against his cheek from the wrong direction. Eljorn started, jerking half out of his meditative posture in surprise. The forest around him was as empty as it had been when he arrived, however, and there was nothing disturbing the natural order.

Settling himself once more, he waited and listened. This new feeling came again, then several more times in rapid succession, falling into a deliberate pattern. He could decipher nothing of these invisible vibrations save the direction from which they came: the clearing where the strange group of men had gone.

Eljorn could hear nothing of the men over the rush of the water, nor could he see them from where he sat, even if he had faced in that direction, but he could *feel* the energy of their activities in much the same way as he saw the sounds of the gong. They must have gone to the clearing at the base of the hill to do… What *were* they doing down there? Was it magic? Followers of Toush were never associated with mysticism, yet the sensations he felt were difficult to attribute to anything else.

He was certainly no expert on the subject, yet their choice of the secluded location was evidence of their need for privacy. His curiosity overrode any worry, and he closed his eyes once more.

So focused was he on evaluating these sensations that he almost missed the timekeeping gong. He hopped to his feet and hurried back to the monastery, wondering how many more mysteries could be revealed by simply sitting in a creek.

* * *

The daily pattern repeated itself for another two weeks, with Eljorn continuing to visit the creek every afternoon and the strange group continuing to ignore him, unworried by his proximity. Their training sessions, for that is what he deduced them to be, became the subject of his mental explorations. Patterns developed quickly, and it was not long before recognizable variations allowed him to determine when the energies were directed away from or towards him in the same way his ears could tell when a sound was approaching or receding.

He ended every session with an attempt of his own at moving or creating those energies, but he possessed a better understanding of how to fly than of how to produce energy out of thin air, and his every effort was fruitless. There was some key understanding of which he was unaware, one in which he lacked even the proper question to frame it. The mystery was a suitable challenge, occupying his every available thought.

Today, however, there would be no opportunity to learn from the strangers. The daily routine was to be set aside for the Hoshinhala Ceremony—a contest of the martial arts coinciding with the graduation of the second-level dimnants to full members of the order. More importantly for Eljorn and the other first levels, its conclusion would mark the end of their period of silence.

He and his fellow dimnants were led out of the monastery complex by one of the instructors not long after lunch, in the opposite direction from his daily wanderings. The day was sunny and warm, and the woods pleasant. A short walk along a manicured path of wide stones brought them to an amphitheater-shaped depression in the hills. The wide area where a stage might have stood had been leveled and covered in a layer of coarse sand, and thick white rope had been stretched between stakes to form a large hexagonal design spanning the center. A small gong flanked by two rows of low padded seats was positioned on the far side. A multitude of monks had arrayed themselves on the grassy slopes, displaying a harmony in the clustering of similar robe colors.

Eljorn and the rest of his group were led partway up the slope, and there they sat shoulder to shoulder in orderly rows. The second levels entered and congregated at the base of the hill. They all had their heads shaved and wore the traditional red robes which would identify them to the world as followers of Toush. It was surprising to see only around twenty men in the group and Eljorn wondered if his own cadre would see similar attrition over the next year.

Without fanfare, the Mantrin and a small cluster of senior monks entered from the base of the arena, escorted by monks dressed as Eljorn had never seen. Their robes were a deep burgundy, over top of which hung chest plates and shoulder guards of lacquered wood and dark leather.

"Shaar," one of the monks behind him whispered, his voice full of awe.

Eljorn had never heard of such a group, though there was

something naggingly familiar about them. There was an air about them that was difficult to name but seemed out of place with the tranquil nature of the services the order rendered, though the disharmony of it was in and of itself somehow proper. What seemed completely out of place was the old monk trailing behind them—the same one Eljorn had seen every evening from his seat in the creek.

The armored men broke formation crisply, each taking station at one of the points of the hexagonal ring. The old man strolled onwards at an unhurried pace and took a seat next to the Mantrin.

"Elder Uncle, who is that with the Mantrin?" Eljorn asked before he could stop himself, the words thick and strange sounding in his own ears after keeping them to himself for so long.

The instructor favored him with a look of disapproval, as the time of silence had not officially ended, but granted him an answer anyway. "That is Hammett."

There was significance to the proclamation, even if exactly what it was remained unknown. Eljorn was filled with questions, but he dared not push his luck further. He had no idea who this Hammett was, but it was clear that he held privileges far above his apparent station.

All in attendance were now seated, and the ceremonial opening proceeded with a lack of pontificating, every participant doing their part in choreographed silence. The contest had been explained to them days before. It was optional but prestigious, open to any of the dimnants of any level. There was nothing for a first-level dimnant to gain from entering, so it remained the purview of the second years. Setting foot in the ring marked one as a combatant, and the goal was to be the last one remaining inside.

Beyond a prohibition on weapons, there were no specific limitations on how one could be ejected from the arena, but all the tenets of Toush applied, as they did in all facets of their lives now, and tradition demanded a certain level of civility. A double tap on the gong called all the participants into the ring.

Around two thirds of the red-robed monks stood and moved towards the ring, opening a grassy path as straight as an arrow from Eljorn's position down to the arena. By luck or happenstance, it aligned directly with where the monk known as Hammett was seated on the far side. The strange monk met his gaze and offered an enigmatic, perhaps inviting, tilt of his head.

Eljorn was on his feet and moving forward before he had time to question the decision. Hammett had already looked away, leaving Eljorn to wonder what he could accomplish by doing this, other than achieve embarrassment as the first one to be tossed from the ring. There was a destination at the end of every path, however, and he was willing to take it on faith, for now.

His entry into the ring was greeted with typical impassivity by those already there, with the other contestants evaluating him in the same way they studied each other. His white first-level robes stood out amongst the reds of the others as they jockeyed for a place near the middle and as far from the edge as possible. Eljorn looked for a place to settle, circling away from obviously stronger opponents. Which, to be fair, was almost all of them. Every one of the men within the ring had the benefit of an entire year's worth of training that he did not.

The gong was struck before he was ready, a hard, sharp blow that crashed through the natural amphitheater, and the ring exploded into action. Two of the closest monks converged on him, likely hoping for an easy elimination. He dove between them, an instinctive reaction more suited to playing with a kennel full of dogs than an adherence to what he had been taught of hand-to-hand combat. It achieved the needed effect, however, as his two would-be assailants suddenly found themselves side-by-side and close to the edge. Eljorn scrambled to his feet as their attention turned from him to each other.

The respite was short lived as another monk came flying at him with a kick meant to take his head off. He ducked beneath it as he blocked. His opponent, a monk of roughly his size, had barely landed before launching into a complex series of attacks. Eljorn tried to keep an awareness of where the edge of the ring was but was stymied at every attempt to retreat from that boundary.

He was surprised when one of the Shaar charged into the ring without warning. Both Eljorn and his opponent jumped away reflexively, though neither seemed the intended target. That dubious honor was reserved for a larger contestant nearby, who had another monk in a chokehold. The Shaar closed the distance far more quickly than his apparent level of effort should have allowed. A nimbus of air rippled around the armored monk, like heat waves on a hot summer day, accelerating and guiding his motions. The Shaar swung both arms in a smooth arc from low to high, gripping the offending contestant midway and lifting him completely from the ground. Ripples of translucent energy swirled from the Shaar's hands as his throw propelled the larger man completely out of the ring in one effortless motion.

That was what they had been practicing in the forest clearing, but this time Eljorn could not only feel what the Shaar was doing, he could see it.

The entire sequence had transpired in the blink of an eye, but Eljorn paid for the momentary diversion of his attention as a red-robed foot crashed into his shoulder. Rather than fight against the blow, he allowed the force of it to send him spinning away, gaining space at the expense of his balance. The maneuver sent him stumbling closer to the edge, just in front of the Shaar who had resumed his station outside the ring.

Eljorn slumped as if he was about to fall, a feigned weakness that his over-eager opponent failed to recognize as he leapt at him with both arms outstretched. Eljorn gripped the man's robes as his foot swung up, sweeping the other monk off balance. He fell with him, using the weight of his own body to pull his opponent completely off his feet and using the momentum of the fall to send the other monk cartwheeling out of the ring.

Directly at the Shaar.

Eljorn watched what happened next from upside down as he continued rolling back to his feet. The instant before the two men collided, the armored monk's legs flew up and back, driven by rippling waves of air. His body straightened for an instant, completely parallel to the ground, then he was twisting, his legs tucked beneath him. He landed as casually as if he had simply hopped over a stick lying on the ground, perfectly balanced on the balls of his feet.

Eljorn returned to his own feet, so excited about the two events he had witnessed that he found himself unable to keep the flicker of a smile from his face. The Shaar met his eyes in shared amusement, then looked at the ground. Eljorn followed his gaze down to where the Shaar's foot was planted just inside the ring.

Realization of what that meant hit Eljorn in the same instant as the Shaar's open palm.

The force of the blow slammed into his chest, sending him flying backwards and almost knocking the wind from his lungs. Eljorn caught the after-trails of rippling air out of the corner of his eye as he tumbled, certain that it was actually directed energy and not the flesh of the monk's hand that had struck him.

A rapid tattoo of punches flew at him unbelievably fast, each accompanied by translucent contrails of energy. The pseudo-premonition gave him just enough forewarning to anticipate where each blow would land, but even with this knowledge, he was able to counter no more than a handful of punches.

Those punches were certainly being pulled to avoid crippling him for life, but even so, it was impossible for him to stand against the onslaught. His own meager defenses seemed to fend off the energy as much as they deflected the physical force of each attack, which provided a glimmer of hope. There was no way for him to produce the energy on his own, but perhaps he could redirect it to his advantage, just as he could use the force of an opponent's attack against him.

Eljorn fell back into a basic kata, feigning confusion. The Shaar's attack came right when he expected, at the weak point of the sequence where both Eljorn's hands were low, the air in front of the monk's fist rippling like the wake from the bow of a boat as it rushed at him. Eljorn threw himself backwards, allowing the strike to land on his shoulder. He seized the energy of the blow, allowing it to twist around him as it spun him in midair. Landing clumsily on his feet, he thrust as much of that energy as he could back towards the Shaar with both hands.

The attempt was unskilled, spilling most of the energy in

unproductive directions, but the rest slammed squarely into the Shaar with an audible slap. The force of it sent him skidding backwards, plowing twin furrows with his feet through the sand. He came to a stop two paces away and remained there, eyes locked on Eljorn's. The pair studied each other, a frozen moment in time broken only when the Shaar winked at him.

Eljorn blinked in surprise, then he was being yanked backwards. Too late, he attempted to counter this new attack, but his feet were already above his head. His vision swirled with glimpses of the sky, red robes, and sand before he met the latter in a jarring impact. He tumbled unceremoniously across the ground, coming to a stop half outside the ring.

Eljorn winced as he pushed himself to his feet, then bowed in the direction of the second-level monk who had tossed him from the ring, though the other man was already on to his next opponent. The Shaar he had sparred with offered him no acknowledgement as he stepped from the ring and resumed his station.

Eljorn stood there breathing heavily, his knees trembling with the effort of keeping him upright. What he had just learned would certainly prove to be worth the effort, but he would have preferred if it had not hurt so much.

* * *

Seven days had passed since the contest. The aches and pains inflicted on Eljorn had finally faded, but the details of what he had seen remained fresh in his thoughts. His studies continued unabated, and if anything they had grown even more strenuous now that verbal communication had been added back in. If his attempt in the arena had made any impact on his instructors or fellow dimnants, none of them had given any indication.

Eljorn continued to make his afternoon visits to the creek, finding his center in its soothing perfection, but of the Shaar and Hammett he had seen no sign.

It was nearing time for him to return from one such visit when he heard footsteps approaching. Eljorn cracked one eye open just enough to see the six Shaar monks approaching, this time climbing back up the hill away from the clearing instead of towards it. They were dressed again in common clothes that gave no hint of their affiliation, but today they carried traveling packs with their weapons. Trailing behind, and still looking very much like a monk of Toush should look, wandered the man known as Hammett.

The troop passed by Eljorn without a word, just as they always did. His eyes opened fully this time as he watched them disappear one by one over the hill. A pang of regret accompanied their leaving, though it was tempered by the knowledge they had unknowingly given him. Sooner or later, Eljorn vowed he would discover the secrets of how they had done it.

Hammett slowed at the crest of the hill, coming to a stop alone in the middle of the trail. He turned to look back at Eljorn over his shoulder, and his weathered face split into a mischievous grin.

"Are you coming?"

A reader once told me that Weeby was "more terrifying than the demons." Our mysterious halfling certainly had a habit of showing up at conspicuously convenient times, and of knowing (and, perhaps, influencing) far more of the goings-on in the world than he should have. That, along with the danger that followed close on the heels of his every appearance, only served to enhance his mystique.

His genesis arose from simple necessity, a needed push to send Tormjere, Gelid, Treven, and those with them speeding into the vast wilderness in pursuit of the Book of Amalthee. When I paused to inquire *why* he was there, and what made him so capable of deftly providing that message, the guise of a simple henchman was stripped away to reveal a complex and contradictory personality.

I remain incapable of revealing all of his secrets, of course, for he has chosen to keep most of them hidden even from me. But the few tales I have coaxed out are incredible, so I can only imagine what all the others may be like.

A Curious Assignment

Weeby skip-stepped ahead, sliding beside a mother and daughter who were walking down the mostly empty street. It was an innocuous action, one which aligned the pair between himself and his overly attentive quarry. One of the great advantages of being a halfling in a world full of taller people was that he could, from a distance, pass for a large child. The blond tint of his hair only added to the effect, as human children tended towards fairer colors that darkened as they grew. The ruse would never hold up to even a casual inspection, no matter how youthful a halfling he was (or still considered himself to be, as evidenced by the upward sweep of his bangs) but, in the correct circumstances, the technique was surprisingly effective.

He set his mind to wandering as aimlessly as his affected attitude might suggest, because the best way to appear uninterested in someone was to legitimately not care about them in the least. It was one of the many skills he had perfected over the years, made easier today by the abundance of other things to occupy his attention. The morning was pleasant, already sunny and bright as a spring day should be but still cooled by both the earliness of the season and the ever-present mists which rose from the town of Fallhaven's namesake waterfall. It was a quaint little village nestled into the base of the forested mountains on the edge of civilization, with the more industrious residents already out and about, getting a jump on the day.

His convenient, if unknowing, companions were doing the same, likely headed to market or perhaps the butcher's. That was what mothers and daughters did in these little towns, wasn't it? Get up first thing in the morning and trundle off to purchase food and sundries for the home while the men set to working their fields or going about their trades. He suspected that the woman had married a man from the former group, as her dress was of linen rather than silk, and she gave no appearance of being wealthy enough to afford a servant to perform the shopping for her.

It was not long before the woman took note of his unacceptable proximity to her daughter, as mothers do, and fixed him with a suspicious eye. He smiled pleasantly at her and shifted his path to drift away from them, just slow enough so as to appear that it was the speed and direction he had been travelling all along, and that she had simply noticed him in passing. She immediately ignored him in a manner that conveyed she was watching him quite closely and wanted nothing more than for him to leave her alone. That was exactly what Weeby did, because when you gave people what they wanted, it was all they would ever see.

Once he had achieved a comfortable distance from them both, he paused at a corner to peruse a baker's wares displayed enticingly in a window, using his movement towards the door to place the building between himself and the small church of Amalthee situated in a grassy field across the street.

That had been close.

Too close, in fact. Either the kid that had almost seen him was unexpectedly lucky or he himself was slipping. Regardless, it made things more interesting, and gods knew that if he was going to traipse all the way to the edges of this little kingdom for something so trivial, he needed to be entertained in the process.

He leaned nonchalantly against the side of the bakery, disappearing into the coolness of the shade even though the warmth of the sun had been more pleasant. Hiding in plain sight was generally the best way to go about this type of surveillance, and the eye had a tendency to skip over dark patches when it was so bright outside.

Judging that sufficient time had passed, he risked a glance back towards the church. The blind old priest that everyone had their robes in a knot over, one Father Gelid, was now speaking with his young… guard? No, the dark-haired boy was too unseasoned for that, especially given the way his sword slapped about awkwardly on his hip. Companion? Guide? He had the look of someone more used to forests than cities and seemed as lost as—

The boy's eyes flicked towards him once more, and Weeby froze, willing his body not to react in any way other than how it had been taught. A slow turn of the head and a gentle unfocusing of the eyes to mask where he had been looking, an idle slouch of his shoulders to disguise the sudden tension in his muscles, a small shuffle of the feet to imply that he was just coming to a rest.

He allowed his gaze to follow a passing wagon and from there along a roofline and then right on up to the waterfall, not daring to look back again.

The young bravo's awareness was unusual, and far more of a challenge than following a doddering old priest and a couple of kids around. While he had not been truly worried, it was still good to know that any potential degradation of his skills was not at fault for the earlier lapse. To be spotted once could be attributed to luck, but twice?

By the time he allowed his attention to wander back towards the church, everyone but the resident priest had disappeared. The clergyman lingered for a moment, facing the direction Gelid, his acolyte, and the strange kid must have gone.

Weeby waited for him to return to his holy duties and then pushed himself away from the wall. They were passing through the town, either because it was the most direct route or perhaps to secure additional supplies. As there were only three roads leaving the town and they had ignored two of them, it meant that Kirchmont was their eventual destination. Armed with that knowledge, Weeby chose a circuitous route outside the city walls towards the unimaginatively named North Gate, from which the group would eventually appear.

He arrived at the exit from the town quickly despite there being no need to rush and settled into a comfortable position beneath a maple tree just coming into its greenness.

The priest was a curious target. Today was the first time Weeby had gotten a good look at him, and he still couldn't understand what all the fuss was about. The old man's blindness and kindly mannerisms were apparent even from a distance, and neither seemed an affectation. He did not present the appearance of a troublemaker, but with priests, as with wizards, one could never be too careful.

Thankfully, Weeby's instructions this time were only to slow his journey long enough to allow other events to unfold. He had partaken in enough unsavory work in this backwoods kingdom of late and focusing on something less taxing was proving to be a pleasant diversion. Given that the trio possessed only a single mule for transportation and might well get lost before reaching the gate he was now watching, that should prove a comically easy task.

Still, he would take nothing for granted. Gelid and his youthful helpers had reached Fallhaven earlier than expected and had taken a very peculiar route to get here. The manner in which they had accomplished it remained a mystery, as the Conclave had lost track of Gelid somewhere along the Gold Road not long after the priest had stepped off a boat in Tythir. Weeby chuckled to himself at that lapse. How embarrassing to lose a blind old man and a child on your very doorstep. It was a mistake he would most certainly *not* repeat.

* * *

Weeby stood scratching his head beneath a very different tree the following morning as he watched the dark-haired youth leading the priest and his acolyte steadily north once more. The grass was still wet and the sun barely enough there to consider the day started, and there they went.

The wrong way.

Yesterday had gone exactly as he expected, with the old man and his young companions taking a laughably long time to reach the thrown together collection of buildings known as the town of Wistran. From here, they should have continued along the well-travelled and well-maintained road as it turned east towards Verone, just like everyone else.

70

What could have possessed them to choose the barely there trail snaking into the wilderness over the much safer road leading east? There were no towns in that direction for days, and his own inquiries the night before had confirmed that it was not uncommon for those who did chance that trail to fall victim to goblins, trolls, or other wild beasts. Gelid had turned daring or foolish, but either way it created problems. Weeby congratulated himself for rising earlier than should have been needed and verifying their direction rather than assuming, but now he desperately needed to get ahead of them.

The options available to him were few.

Should he take the same path, there would be almost no way to pass them unnoticed, and he did not have the time or desire to attempt going off trail to leapfrog ahead. Their route was likely to cut three or four days from their expected journey, and even were he to acquire a horse and race along the traditional road—something he was already resigned to doing—that would be unacceptably close. Iferion had to be in Kirchmont by now, and Gelid's early arrival was sure to disrupt whatever the wizard was supposed to be doing at the abbey there.

Stepping behind the tree to block the view of anyone from the village who might be looking, Weeby pulled a dohedron from an inner pocket. He possessed three of the rare signaling devices—a mark of some pride, given that few were allowed even one. His fingers danced across the gems embedded in the multi-facetted device like a musician's on a flute, each stone pulsing with light as it was tapped in a coded sequence.

Priest will arrive three days soonest.

It was hardly an elegant sentence, but he was in a hurry and it was the best he could achieve with the twelve-sided device.

There was a longer than usual delay and he began to wonder if he would be forced to repeat himself. Thank the gods the wizard was an early riser, however, as the gems flickered their multi-hued response.

Felzig not here. Delay.

Weeby rolled his eyes at the obviousness of that statement and returned the dohedron to his pocket without bothering to reply. Of course he was going to delay them. The question remained how.

The most convenient, if unlikely, solution was to hope that the ill-prepared travelers would be waylaid by beasts along the dangerous road. Trusting in the fates for a random encounter to solve his problem was hardly a plan, however. He could try to force such a situation, but attempting to find and bargain with the less civilized creatures of the world was always dicey, and there was no call for so gruesome an outcome.

All that was truly needed was to slow them down, and his easiest lever would be the mule, though that too posed a challenge. He could follow and dispose of the beast in the night but harming the animal would be both distasteful and unimaginative, and it carried more risk of discovery than was justified. If it were to be stolen, on the other hand…

With that sliver of a plan in mind, he hurried back to where the clerics had spent the night.

The tavern gave every appearance of being a better run stopover than the seedier one he had been forced to bed down at—there was at least a serving bar here instead of just a keg propped atop a rickety table—but that was a relative evaluation. Either establishment would have been relegated to the slums of a reputable city.

He found what he was looking for almost immediately: a trio of disheveled men slumped over a table in the corner. Every public drinking house attracted the same sorts, and the less imaginative among them had proven quite useful in the past, under the right circumstances.

The innkeep was asleep atop a stool behind the bar, his arm slung protectively over a pair of tall wooden boxes.

"Mornin'," Weeby rasped, stifling a pretend yawn of his own.

The man opened one eye halfway but did not stir from his seat.

"I'll take two bottles of whatever they were drinking last night," Weeby said, affecting a sleepy and unrefined voice. "Must've been good, an' I need it."

The innkeep gave him a dubious look but rousted himself enough to lift the rotting top of one of the boxes and reach inside. Such a herculean effort was accompanied by grunts and groans, but he eventually produced a pair of bottles.

Weeby slid four Kingdom coins across the stained wood, intentionally underpaying.

"Four ships each," the innkeep said in a gravelly voice typical of those who had breathed too much smoke for too many years.

Weeby looked pained as he pulled more coins from his almost-empty purse. It was all for show, as he carried enough wealth secreted about his person to buy the entire village, but appearances were everything. "How about seven so I can still eat tonight?"

The innkeep swept the coins away with an inarticulate noise of acceptance and settled ungracefully back onto his stool.

Even though trouble was unlikely, Weeby evaluated his avenues of escape as he shuffled nonchalantly towards the oblivious ruffians, who had no idea what they were about to volunteer for. His path to the door was clear, and one of the nearby windows was sufficiently open for him to leap through. He had been forced to do that often enough to know he would fit. A fire poker leaned against a wall, within easy reach, should it come to that.

"Mornin'," he said dejectedly as he collapsed onto the bench across the table from the three men.

The big one lifted his head just enough to see who was talking and gave a grunt, which was apparently how people here chose to communicate this early in the day.

Weeby hid one bottle beneath the table as he set the other squarely between them. The man's bleary eyes struggled to focus on it as Weeby poured himself a cup, though the other two remained unresponsive.

"Wanna share a drip with those down on their luck?" the big man mumbled, pushing himself upright.

"Always willing to hoist a cup with a fellow working man," Weeby said, "unlike those priests of Amalthee."

"Mungo saw 'em."

The man's breath was as rancid as meat left in the sun for a week, and if he was referring to himself in the third person then last night's binge must have been *really* good. Weeby dumped some of the bitter-smelling liquid into another cup and shoved it towards Mungo.

"Can't stand how they treat us," Weeby said, resting his head in his hands in feigned misery. "Makes my head hurt."

"What'd they do t' you?"

"Took our family mule," Weeby said. "Stole it right away for something they didn't do, and just 'cause they could."

The statement would have been almost incoherent to a man of clear thought, but Mungo was far from sober and probably not that bright when he was.

He finally gathered himself enough to empty his cup with one swallow. "They're always stealin', and don't help nobody."

"Yeah. They've got all the money. Why do they need more?"

"Greedly," Mungo agreed, thumping his fist on the table.

There was such solemn fervor in the declaration that Weeby struggled not to laugh at the mispronunciation. He refilled Mungo's cup. "Wish I could go take it back, but I just can't," he moaned, watching the big man's eyes glaze as the possibilities slowly sank in.

"Should do somethin' about that."

"That would be just what they deserve. You could even keep the mule for yourself."

Mungo tossed down another drink, and his grin became unbalanced. "Yeah, I could. Maybe he'll lose more than just that."

"Nothing too drastic," Weeby cautioned. "He's not the one that stole it. I just want them to pay what's due to me."

"Take the mule and make 'em suffer the walk. That'll show 'em."

"Justice!" Weeby agreed, passing the half-empty bottle to Mungo, who skipped the cup completely this time as he took a swig.

"We'll take the mule an' ride it all the way to Kirchmont!" Mungo declared theatrically to his comatose companions. "Won't be stuck here no more."

"And the glories of that city will greet your arrival," Weeby affirmed. Gods, drunks were so stupid. "My family will be indebted to you for this. It's not much, but here's another bottle you can keep for luck."

Mungo heaved his bulk from the bench and smacked the other two awake. After continuous and forceful encouragement, both boys dragged themselves to their feet sullenly, none too pleased at having been woken.

Weeby trailed behind the inebriated men as they staggered from the tavern, giving them a nudge to make sure they took the correct road. The looming run-in might not end well for the good Father, but a little highway robbery would not draw the least bit of attention. Given how loud Mungo was now singing, he and his cronies would likely be too drunk to cause serious damage, anyway.

It was far from his best work, but he put it out of his mind. He needed to get himself to Kirchmont before Gelid and his boys showed up, and that meant days and nights of racing the long way around.

"Now," he said to himself with a sigh, "where can I find a horse?"

* * *

A week and a half later, Weeby concluded that his fortunes were not improving. He was propped casually against a weathered and warped fence, wedged into the shadowy corner between the dilapidated arrangement of loose wooden slats meant to enclose a sad little garden and the equally decrepit building to which both were attached. The stagnant, wet air was thick enough to cut with a knife, but the blade in his hand was employed more productively at working a piece of wood—an affectation of idleness he had actually grown to enjoy over the years. It was the only pleasant thing to be found amongst the dirty hovels and disreputable denizens of Evermen's Forge, and he wished for the hundredth time that he could have stayed in Kirchmont.

The day had dawned cloudy and dark, thankfully absent of the rainy deluge that had soaked everything of late but nevertheless wet and cheerless. At least things were about to get more interesting.

Felzig and his troop had arrived at this blemish in the middle of the vast forest just the day before—with the priest, for some reason—and it was only a matter of time before they came looking for him. He couldn't decide if it was more surprising that they had made it here so fast or that they had made it here at all, given that little arrangement that had been awaiting them on the road, and he was more than a bit curious as to how it had been accomplished.

Almost on cue, a voice reached his ears from beyond the fence: "What did you find out?"

Weeby chuckled just loud enough for the sound to carry through the gaps of the wooden barrier. "That isn't the proper code word."

"To the hells with code words; I don't have time," Joloff shot back. "Where is he?"

The swordsman from the Conclave's protective arm never had time—or patience—for a reasonable conversation, but Weeby supposed that just went with the profession.

"Iferion left with it last night," Weeby said, "as soon as he realized you were close. He headed due west, alone."

Joloff swore, which only increased Weeby's amusement with the whole situation.

"If it makes you feel better, he wasn't any happier about it than you are. You know how he hates dealing with goblins."

"If he'd done a better job with the ambush, he wouldn't be

alone," Joloff shot back in disgust.

Weeby winced. "Goblins lack an understanding of the subtleties required for this kind of work, but I went to considerable effort to make them understand what was required. I even had to divide all the coins by appearance rather than weight so none of them felt cheated. What happened?"

Joloff shifted against the other side of the fence as he watched the street. "Thought it was too well designed for a wizard. It started out good enough. I had everyone nicely separated, with our defense overloaded on the uphill side. The priests were unprotected from behind."

"And?"

"And that cursed kid wiped out the entire second group that was sneaking in."

"All of them?" Weeby said, impressed.

"With a dagger rammed through his side, no less."

"It almost sounds like you're starting to like him."

"I'm not, but his skills are… unexpected."

Weeby filed that away. It was difficult to impress a man like Joloff, especially when he did not like you to begin with. "Does the old man really need to die for this to work?"

"Felzig wants them killed, but it's got to look natural."

Weeby sighed. Felzig would say that, wouldn't he?

Their conversation paused as a knot of men passed close.

"So, what shall I do for you?" Weeby asked when the group was out of earshot.

"We're supposed to be chasing Iferion. Stupid kid's off poking around like he'll actually discover something on his own. Give the little snot a shove to get us going in the right direction before the priest decides to turn back to Kirchmont and get help. I'll take it from there."

Weeby scratched his chin thoughtfully. "You want to chase Iferion further into the wilderness? What does Felzig think of that idea?"

"Opinions are irrelevant. We each have a job to do, even if we have to wander in these stupid woods for a month to do it."

Weeby almost laughed at the notion. The stiffly proper wizard would hate any amount of time in these forested mountains—there was dirt here. "So we do. It would still be easier to just toss them off a cliff."

"Someone we don't control has to see it and live to tell others."

"Ah, that's why you have those two Irdrians. I thought you just wanted some fodder to make the ambush more believable."

Joloff made a dismissive sound. "They're useless idiots like the rest of their countrymen, but they gossip like a pair of old women."

"And what if our young swordsman figures you out?"

Joloff was a thorough man who would have already planned for that contingency, but it was fun to poke at him under the guise of looking out for his wellbeing.

"I'll keep Felzig safe from the boy," Joloff said. "Right now, I need to go retrieve that idiot acolyte before he gets himself offed in town." The boards of the fence shifted as he straightened.

"Joloff?"

The man paused.

"Be careful around the boy. There's something peculiar about him."

"I'll give him enough rope to hang himself with. We'll see what he does with it."

Weeby sat shaking his head as Joloff's footsteps receded. The problem with handing a man a noose was that he could just as easily turn around and use it on you.

Introduction to
"A Sacred Duty"

I have been asked, on occasion, as to which character in this series is my favorite. It's a query that is impossible to answer, a bit like trying to select a favorite child. Each is unique, and I am attached to them all in different ways and for different reasons. But my favorite character to *write* is, without question, Enna.

Specifically, angry Enna.

She is a woman fiercely passionate in her beliefs, with a fiery temper to match, and she has never been reluctant to make her viewpoint known. Her verbal battles with Tormjere, and the intensity and frequency with which they occurred, have been a source of endless amusement over the years. Yet it is her love for, and commitment to, both Tormjere and Shalindra that defines her true nature.

The relationship that the three would share was hinted at in only the vaguest of manners, guided by an unseen hand long before any of them were born. The sacrifices made by Tormjere and Shalindra would prove staggering in their enormity, yet no more costly and debilitating than the ones Enna endured to be there for them.

Hers was a journey fraught with its own perils and filled with more than its share of predicaments. Yet it, like that of so many others, transpired exactly as it was meant to.

A Sacred Duty

Soft shadows rippled across her fingers as Enna cinched the drawstring tight on her travelling bag, sealing inside it her few worldly possessions. Morning sunlight filtered past the canopy of leaves outside and streamed through the cozy room's single window, warming the air and brightening the rich grain of the polished wooden walls. She brushed a long strand of perfectly white hair behind the pointed tip of her ear and allowed her gaze to trace along the intricate pattern of knots and whorls in the wood, a calming path she had memorized over decades of observation. Today, the exercise proved fruitless.

Taking a breath to steady her rapidly beating heart, she looped the bag over her shoulder. It hung there lightly, its inconsequential bulk made up almost entirely of a thin cloak and a spare robe, white and sleeveless like the one she wore. There were no personal trinkets or memorabilia to weigh it down. The only adornment she allowed herself was the intricately engraved, pure silver disc of Elurithlia, goddess of the moon, which hung as it always did from a silver chain around her neck.

She opened the door to leave, but, uncharacteristically, she paused at the threshold to take one more look at this space which had sheltered her for so long. It seemed a needlessly melodramatic action. This place would still be waiting for her when she returned, after all. Shrugging aside such thoughts, she stepped from the room and made her way down the hall.

The multilevel dormitory was home to hundreds of elvish Sisters of Elurithlia, and the corridor was bustling with people. Despite all the activity, the building's solid wooden construction swallowed sound, lending it a quiet, contemplative air well aligned with its purpose. Most of the women were returning from the morning prayer—the one that Enna had missed—or were headed to break their nightly fast and begin their day. The majority were transient, coming to study and pray at the temple forest in the capital city of Eitholmir, the most holy site in not only the elvish nation of Ildalarial but indeed all the world.

The Sisters who recognized her offered a cheerful smile or a quick embrace, in the elvish custom. The reactions of those who had never seen her before were just as pleasant but far more curious; there was not an elf alive who possessed the green eyes and straight, pure white hair that Enna did, nor had there been for centuries. The woman she so closely resembled—Illathalirial, the most powerful Guardian to have ever been—had unknowingly influenced so much of her life. Despite the attention, the time was long past when she would have been self-conscious of her appearance. There was purpose to the gift of fate that signaled the favor of her goddess Elurithlia, and recent events only lent credence to the destiny she had been promised all her life.

She allowed her hand to trail along the railing as she swiftly descended a curving flight of stairs towards the ground floor, her fingers recognizing every blemish in a surface worn smooth by millennia of elvish fingers. A turn to the left and a few dozen steps carried her to a pair of carved doors, and then she was outside. The routine mechanics of her journey from room to exit helped settle her anticipation of what was to come.

As with every public building in the city of Eitholmir, the imposing expanse of the dormitory was surrounded by well-tended gardens meant to soften and embrace the structure, and the path from door to street wound back and forth in curving lines through a lush carpet of color and greenery. The early spring flowers were in bloom, and the air was filled with the buzz of pollinators as they went about their duties. The butterflies flitting about the garden matched the giddy excitement swirling in her stomach, even though this would be far from her first journey beyond Ildalarial's borders.

Trilaria awaited her at the end of the path, hopping on her toes with anticipation. Hair the color of autumn leaves bounced about her shoulders, and a smile that could infect an entire room split her face as she caught sight of Enna.

"I thought I would have to come wake you," Trilaria said, her sleeveless white robes fluttering as she skipped forward to embrace her warmly.

"Only because you're impatient," Enna answered with a smile of her own. It was impossible not to be happy around her. Trilaria was the kind of woman who could chastise you for the most egregious sin and somehow leave you feeling thankful she had done so by the time she was finished. Born just days apart, the two were sisters in everything but name, and closer than any siblings come from the same parents.

Trilaria grabbed her hand and practically dragged her across the broad thoroughfare separating the dormitory from the temple forest. "You know they're all waiting for us."

Enna's eyes flicked left along the treeline towards the mostly obscured path which led to Lana Ariiliar, the Glade of Guardians. She considered visiting that sacred space one more time before leaving, but they were already plunging through one of the wide, wooded tunnels into Lana Clariandar, the Glade of Worship. The gigantic field, ringed by mighty trees, could and regularly did accommodate thousands of the faithful. Despite being the most public space within the temple forest, it was devoid of any altar or artifact. Only a slight rise at the far side allowed the Sisters leading any given ritual to be seen from everywhere within the glade.

Despite its recent use for the morning prayer, the clearing was empty now save for a small group of elves who waited next to a cluster of horses. A stranger to their culture might have been surprised at the presence of animals within their worship space, but elves retained their connection to the natural world far more closely than the other races. Enna almost laughed as she imagined the effect of animals inside the sanctuary of a human temple.

"What's so funny?" Trilaria asked.

Trilaria had spent as much time as she had in the human kingdoms and would appreciate the humor of it, but they were already close to everyone, and Enna thought it best not to share with those who would be less understanding. She demurred with a gentle shake of her head.

Trilaria gave her hand a small squeeze, releasing it as her parents, the two least official people there, cheerfully descended on them. There were excited hugs and well-wishes all around, but as much as Enna wished to linger within the warmth of her surrogate family, she quickly disengaged.

Three men in the muted greens and browns of the Woodswardens stood watch near the horses, already fulfilling their role as escorts despite the sanctity of their current location. Four members of the Grand Calontier were here as well, each resplendent in their most formal attire. Yet it was the last woman present who held Enna's attention. Elothlirial, her birth mother and Manalathlia of all who worshiped the moon, stood slightly apart from everyone else, waiting for Enna to draw near.

"You were absent from the morning prayer," her mother said reproachfully in a voice meant only for Enna.

"I felt a quiet place was more appropriate for my devotions today."

"It might have been," her mother said, taking her by the elbow and steering her farther away from the others, "but leadership often requires us to be visible even when we do not wish to be. At no time in our lives has this ever been more important. The Guardian's Prophecy is imminent, and your destiny is at hand."

Enna cast a fleeting glance over her shoulder at Trilaria. "As long as one of us Ascends, I will be happy."

Elothlirial lifted a slender hand and ran her delicate fingers down Enna's hair, admiring it as a jeweler might regard her finest work. "Elurithlia blessed you above all others, from your appearance to your unwavering devotion and aptitude for channeling divinity. I have prayed every day since your birth that you would be everything She needs you to be, and I am as certain of Her answer as I have ever been. When you reunite Alta Suralia with Her holy armor, you will achieve the destiny you were marked for at birth. Do not doubt."

"I will never doubt Her."

"Are you prepared?"

There were layers to that question, as there always were. "I am as ready as I can be, and confident that we are doing Her will."

"Good." Elothlirial beckoned all of those in the clearing to join them.

The Woodswardens were fastest to cross the open space, almost as eager as Trilaria. The senior man, Ilyand, had performed numerous duties for the temple over the years and was one of her mother's favorites to call upon. He would serve as the Valtilaniar, the one responsible for their safety at all times. Valken she knew by name alone, while the third man she had never seen, yet she held no doubts as to his capabilities. All fell into respectful silence as her mother began to speak.

"You are all aware of the significance of what you are about to undertake. After decades of negotiations, Alta Suralia at last makes its way home. The blood moon has appeared in the west as was foretold, and the time of the Guardian approaches once more. It is for this purpose alone that you will escort Her sacred implement on the final steps of its journey. Do not allow anything or anyone to sway you from this result."

It was Ilyand who answered. "We will see it done no matter what the humans may foist upon us."

Trilaria shared a surprised glance with Enna. "Surely, you don't expect any subterfuge. Not after the accords."

"They have broken agreements before, Revered Sister," Ilyand said. "We will do what we must."

"Humans are not all bad," Enna protested. "No matter how crude their ceremonies, many of their hearts are good."

"Have caution with your sympathies," her mother warned. "We must never forget the events which brought us to this point and necessitated our chosen course of action. The betrayal that took the life of our last Guardian and allowed Elurithlia's weapon to be stolen by the humans can at last be rectified. We are righting a wrong, and nothing must be allowed to prevent that."

There was truth to that. A dwarf was said to have committed the vile deed, but humans had leapt at the opportunity to abscond with what was not theirs.

Regardless, all this talk of trouble was clearly distressing to Trilaria's parents, so Enna steered towards a more soothing outcome. "Elurithlia will keep us safe, and events will transpire as She wills them," she said, before anyone could comment further. "Manalathlia, if we might receive your blessing before we depart?"

Her mother nodded, giving her a glance of approval for her control of the conversation.

Enna knelt with the others, her fingers wrapping comfortably around the silver disc of her faith.

Elothlirial raised a hand as she prayed. "Elurithlia, we ask that you shelter these faithful as they seek to fulfill your holy desires. Keep them safe from hardship and give them strength to carry out your blessed purpose. Send them forth to triumph, in your light."

The words filled Enna with purpose. No matter what might happen, she would see the will of her goddess fulfilled.

By your light, Elurithlia, it will be so.

* * *

"Merrywood," Ilyand said, pointing across the river.

Enna looked with dismay towards the handful of weathered buildings clustered on the narrow road that ran along the far bank. Merrywood was a supposed bastion of cohabitation between elves and humans along a border that was almost entirely in dispute, but Enna's travels had, surprisingly, avoided the town before now. After three days of riding that had carried them northeast through elvish lands with wooded villages and pleasant hostels, it was difficult to believe that this was all that awaited them. "*That* is where people live?"

Trilaria laughed. "I thought the same the first time I saw it. The town is set off the road, as is proper."

Ilyand did not join in their mirth, instead glancing around the woods nervously. He had been doing that a lot. "Come. Let's cross quickly."

They led their horses one at a time over the river via a narrow wooden bridge that swayed more than it should have, then they remounted and bypassed the dilapidated structures. A short road wound eastward through the woods before depositing them into the town proper, where her opinion of the place improved. The homes and shops lining the road were orderly and neat, an odd but still pleasing blend of elvish and human design. While not as heavily wooded as a typical elvish village, the natural world retained an acceptable foothold amongst the buildings.

The size of everything was just a shade too large, as it always was in the human world. Humans were taller than most elves by a head and thicker through the torso. With that added size came added energy, and Enna had discovered early on that they rarely sat still long enough to enjoy anything. Her time in Fallhaven last year had allowed her to experience other amusing shortcomings of human society, from their overly repressed emotions to their occasionally nonsensical social customs.

Side streets branched off here and there, but Ilyand made only one turn as he led them to the temple of Elurithlia.

The building was constructed of white marble instead of retaining the freedom of an open glade, but at least its central hall was round instead of the unpleasantly sharp rectangles that dominated human architecture. Why they liked to obscure the sky behind solid stone would always be a mystery to her.

Their approach was noted by the Sister standing at the open doorway, and by the time they arrived an older human woman was there to greet them at the top of the steps.

"Welcome once more to Merrywood," she said, smiling warmly.

Trilaria hopped from her horse and rushed up the steps to give the woman a hug. "Sister Ippelia, it's so good to see you again! This is Sister Enna."

Ippelia bowed her head to Enna. "It is an honor to meet you." She turned her attention to the Woodswardens. "Ilyand, you remember where the horses go. Join us when you're done."

"Thank you, Revered Sister," he replied. "We shall."

"It's good that you are here," Ippelia said to the two women, her demeanor turning serious. "But what we must discuss is best not done on the streets. Come."

The doorway opened directly into the worship hall, and from there they followed her down a narrow corridor to a small, austere chamber that was likely her personal room.

"I wish I had better news," Ippelia said, "but word reached us just yesterday that the whereabouts of our Sisters who carry

Shinning Moon is not known. We believe them to have been swept up in the fighting."

"That's terrible!" Trilaria exclaimed.

Enna was stunned by the sudden declaration. "What fighting? Have we any idea where?"

"You wouldn't know, of course," Ippelia said. "The kingdoms of Actondel and Ceringion make war again, as they are prone to do every so often. We hear rumors of conflict almost every year, but it seems to be true this time."

Enna fought down the hollow feeling in her stomach. "How close are our Sisters?"

"They were known to have crossed the Small Sea and arrived in Actondel, but they were days overdue in Halisford. Beyond that, we know little. I wish I was able to provide you with more."

"Thank you for all that you have done," Enna said. "Is the road to Fallhaven still safe?"

"The battles are far to the east, so it should be free of trouble. I do pray that Her weapon makes it there swiftly. Oh, to think that another Ascension could take place so soon after the last."

"We will do all that we can to make that happen," Enna said.

Ippelia gave an apologetic smile. "May you do so in Her light. You must be weary, and I thank you for hearing me out immediately. Let me show you to your room, so we may at least ease your burdens for a time."

The room was just down the hall, an uncluttered space containing two double bunks and a small table. Ippelia excused herself, leaving the two elves alone.

"Can you believe it?" Trilaria asked. "After all these years, someone has to start a war right when Alta Suralia is finally coming home."

"We'll still see it home," Enna said, though she had no idea how that would be accomplished.

A polite knock at the door announced Ilyand's arrival, and Trilaria welcomed him in.

He entered only far enough to close the door behind himself and maintained as respectful a distance as possible from the two women.

"Sister Ippelia told me what has happened," he said. "I'm not surprised. May I ask what you intend to do now?"

"I feel we should continue to Fallhaven," Enna answered. "These reports could be in error."

Trilaria nodded. "If they have not resurfaced by the time we get there, we can retrace their intended route until something presents itself."

Ilyand looked worried. "If I may suggest another path, Revered Sisters? There are indications that the goblin tribes may move against Actondel from the mountains between Ildalarial and Silvalaria. If true, the road to Fallhaven cuts across their likely path. Were we to go first to Gyland, then travel overland north by east until reaching the Yarrowonli River and Halisford, we might reach them sooner and avoid the danger."

The places he spoke of were nothing but names on a map to Enna and seemed impossibly far away. Yet many elves, and even Guardians, had travelled farther still.

"A goblin incursion would have been perilous to our intended route," she pointed out. "If you knew of this possibility, why would we have gone that way to begin with?"

"We have contingencies in place to keep you safe."

Enna crossed her arms. "I fail to see how three of you would protect us from an army of goblins."

Ilyand fidgeted uncomfortably. "There are additional forces hidden outside Fallhaven to protect us if needed."

"How many?"

He hesitated. "Fifty."

"We have a war party here in Actondel?" Trilaria asked in surprise.

Ilyand motioned for her to keep her voice down. "We're prepared for any eventuality, Revered Sister. It is my duty to protect both the artifact and you."

"An invasion would be a risk to us all," Enna said. "We should at least warn the humans of the danger."

"Let our enemies weaken each other," he scoffed. "We are not here to save them, and it would be a violation of our treaties to have so many men within their borders. Their own scouts should warn them of the danger. Whether we continue to Fallhaven or turn for Halisford is your choice, Revered Sister. I may only present options."

Enna glanced at Trilaria.

"Your mother put you in charge," Trilaria said, helpfully pointing out the obvious.

Enna gave her an unamused frown. "Only because she likes me better, not because I *am* better."

"True, and don't you forget it," Trilaria teased, her eyes sparkling. "But it is still your decision. Either choice has merit, and both carry substantial risk."

Enna was torn, but Elurithlia's holy relic was in danger, and they could not rely on fate to keep it safe. "We will make for

Halisford and do all that we can to locate Alta Suralia. It cannot be lost again."

"If you'll excuse me then, I'll make ready," Ilyand said. "It may take a day or two to resupply." He bowed and departed the room.

Trilaria placed a hand on Enna's shoulder as she stood. "It's the right choice."

Enna placed her own hand over Trilaria's in thanks, praying that it would be so.

* * *

The wisdom of her decision had been called into question at least a hundred times by the time the city of Halisford came into view. Their travels across the middle of Actondel had been miserable, at least any time they came close to civilization, having been treated with disdain and sometimes outright hostility at each stop and made to feel unwelcome everywhere in between. Ilyand and the other Woodswardens had been forced to draw weapons twice, and it was only by Elurithlia's mercy that neither time had come to bloodshed. The relationship between this nation and hers had never been idyllic, but something seemed to have worked the humans into a frenzy. Only when the road became narrow and the settlements sparse were they able to let their guard down.

The countryside they had traversed had been beautiful and often wild, but the sprawling mass of buildings before them was like a cancerous blight that had consumed everything green beneath stone and smoke. They could not see the waters of River Yarrowonli, as the city sat atop the edge of a narrow canyon, nor could they hear its pleasing roar over the commotion of the place.

Judging from the disorganized mess of people streaming from the city, Enna could only assume that their poor luck would continue. Soldiers were everywhere along the battlements, and people rushed in and out of the city, clogging the gates. The knot of soldiers off to the side of the gates fixed the elves with distrustful looks, but Ilyand timed their entry just as a wagon was between the two groups, and no attempt to stop them was made.

It was more chaotic inside the walls than out, and even from atop their horses it was difficult to forge their way through the crowds. Enna became disoriented after the second turn, but Ilyand led them unerringly towards the white marbled temple of Elurithlia.

A low wall surrounded the gardens arrayed before it, though the opening in the decorative barrier was ungated. They dismounted, and the Woodswardens took command of the horses.

"I don't like this at all," Ilyand said. "I don't know what's afoot, but we should not linger."

Trilaria appeared equally unsettled. "I agree."

"We'll see what our Sisters know," Enna said. She and Trilaria hurried down the broad path towards the temple.

The rectangular building was of typically human construction, all in white marble beneath a low-peaked roof, and a row of smooth columns across the façade. Enna was surprised to find the doors closed and locked, and in the absence of a knocker she thumped on them with her fist.

After a few minutes, a muffled voice carried through the door. "How may we help you?"

"I am Sister Enna, just arrived here with Sister Trilaria from Ildalarial. We—"

There was a clank as the bolt was thrown. The door jerked open halfway, and a white-robed woman peeked her head out.

"Elves! Bless you both for risking the streets. Inside, quickly!"

"What of our escort?" Enna asked.

The woman looked past Enna to where the Woodswardens waited with the horses, then pointed up the street as she called out, "The closest stable is two blocks that way."

Ilyand took one look in that direction and shook his head, then yelled back. "If we leave the horses we'll probably never get them back. We'll wait here."

Enna waved her agreement, and she followed Trilaria and the other woman inside.

The interior of the temple was cool and quiet, its sanctuary dominated by a large statue of Elurithlia standing at the opposite end. A small fountain bubbled a calming tone at the statue's feet, but the Sisters moving about were clearly agitated and their steps hurried.

"What's going on?" Enna asked their guide.

The woman wrung her hands as she led them across the worship chamber. "We are to be put under siege. I'm told that they're locking the gates tonight."

Reaching the far wall, she opened a door and ushered them into a small sitting room. "Sister Superior Denella will want to speak to you immediately. Please wait here, and I'll get her."

"This is insanity," Trilaria said when they were alone.

Enna plopped onto a cushioned bench in frustration. "Is there any part of this kingdom that isn't a disaster?"

It was not long before the Sister Superior came to join them, closing the door to the room securely behind her. Denella was a thin woman whose hair had almost entirely gone to grey, but time had yet to dim the clarity of her stern gaze.

Enna rose and bowed respectfully. "We are so glad to meet you."

"The honor is mine," Denella replied. "It is rare for elves to visit us, but I believe that I know what purpose brought you here."

"We seek Alta— Shining Moon," Enna said. "Have you seen it or heard from those who carry it?"

Denella shook her head. "I believe it was close to the city not a week prior, but it did not visit our temple."

Enna was crushed. Had she made the wrong choice? If the weapon had reached Fallhaven by now, how long would it remain there waiting on them?

"Do you know who carries it now?" Trilaria asked. "Or where it has been taken?"

"A Sister Kayala safeguards it," Denella answered. "Word was delivered to us by written message that she was within the army of Actondel, called to that place to give aid to those wounded in the campaign. It was hastily written and intentionally cryptic, but I understood its true meaning. I disposed of the note immediately, questioning the wisdom of such a missive. But now that you are here, it is clear that Eluria guided Kayala's hand."

"We are fortunate to have been given any direction," Enna agreed. "At least we have a name, and a place to look."

It was certainly a dangerous turn of events, and a seemingly bizarre choice for this Kayala to have made. Enna briefly feared that her mother might have been correct and the humans were still trying to keep the hammer to themselves, but she shook the thought aside.

"The hospitality of Her temple is at your disposal," Denella said, "though I fear you have no time to avail yourself of it. If we become besieged, it may be weeks before anyone can leave."

"Will you be safe here?" Trilaria asked.

"Eluria will watch over us, as She always does, but you must hurry away. I pray her blessings follow you as well."

"We will leave immediately," Enna said. "Thank you."

Denella followed as they hurried to the temple door. "Stay strong in Her light."

The sun was low in the sky as they emerged, and Ilyand was halfway through the gardens, apparently coming to retrieve them.

"Revered Sisters," he said urgently as they descended the steps. "We must depart at once or we may become trapped here."

"We were told of the siege," Trilaria said. "There is—"

"We don't have time now," Ilyand cut her off. "This city is about to become a prison. The gate we entered to the south is our closest way out."

"What we seek lies north, across the river," Enna said.

Ilyand bit off whatever curse he wanted to utter and broke into a jog, speeding them towards the waiting mounts. "It's days in either direction to find a ford. Are you certain?"

"As certain as we can be of anything," Enna said, matching his pace.

"Then we've no choice but to risk traversing the city. We must ride swiftly. Do not allow yourself to slow, even should you trample someone."

They leapt upon the waiting horses. Enna took one last look at the temple, seeing Denella standing at the door. She waved in farewell, praying that Elurithlia would keep them safe in the coming days.

The group forged a meandering route through the crowded

streets. Ilyand grew increasingly nervous at their slow pace and was forced to ask for directions more than once, though his requests for aid were ignored as often as not.

As the sun dipped below the rooftops, throwing deep shadows across the already unfamiliar streets, Enna felt a stab of panic, fearing that they had dallied too long at the temple. She was thoroughly turned around, but Ilyand's sense of direction was true, bringing them onto a wide thoroughfare aimed directly at the fortress. Their next turn to the right placed them on a similarly broad street with the gatehouse in view.

Once free of the walls and across the river, they spurred their horses to a gallop, racing through the deepening dusk without slowing until they reached a forested area several miles from the city. Ilyand found a spot away from the road on the far side of a hill to make camp, and they ate a cold dinner in silence, pondering the events of the day.

"Look there," Ilyand said, pointing.

Enna turned with Trilaria to follow his finger towards an orange glow spread across the eastern horizon.

"Campfires?" she asked.

Ilyand nodded grimly. "The Ceringion army. This place is not safe, Revered Sisters. Though I do not put faith in these human roads at night, I trust an army of conquest even less. Their scouts may already be close."

"Our Sister who carries Alta Suralia was last known to have joined the army of Actondel."

"What?" Ilyand asked in disbelief.

"We don't know why," Enna said. "All we were given was a name."

He clenched his fist. "They are trying to steal it again."

"The message was incomplete," Enna cautioned, "but sent by someone who wanted to be found."

"I believe that is true," Trilaria said, "but I still cannot understand what would possess this Sister Kayala to join their army."

Enna shrugged. "We can only assume she felt safer there."

"Or they've changed their minds," Ilyand said in disgust. "This whole kingdom seems to be falling apart."

"Regardless," Enna said, "we need to get to Alta Suralia, no matter what obstacles are before us. If that means tracking down this kingdom army, so be it."

"Finding their legions will be child's play, Revered Sister," Ilyand said. "Protecting you from them will be significantly harder."

"Elurithlia will not lead us astray. As Alta Suralia goes, so shall we follow."

* * *

Four days passed before they located the kingdom army, which they found engaged with a force of Ceringion invaders. Two more days were taken as they skirted the fighting to find the safest way into the Kingdom camp. In the end, they opted to enter from the rear with the rest of the camp followers. Enna had feared for any number of horrible outcomes but drifting into the camp had proven surprisingly easy. Armies on the move were spread over a lot of ground, she discovered, and so Ilyand and the other Woodswardens found no difficulty in dodging their patrols. They simply waited for the opportune moment and melted into the long train of followers spread behind the combatants.

Their presence was less contentious than it had been in many of the towns, perhaps due to the needs of so many. She and Trilaria were approached almost instantly to mend broken bones or inspect cuts and bruises, and they were given coins and food in thanks. She thought it odd that there were not more women of Elurithlia here to attend to the injured, but there was no making sense of anything related to this war.

In their efforts of caring for the wounded, they crossed paths with Ascerlon, a mediturgeon who made frequent forays amongst the tents of the camp followers. Enna thanked Elurithlia for this stroke of fortune, as the healer was familiar with all who cared for the sick and injured, and he offered to escort Enna and Trilaria to see Sister Kayala. Ilyand had almost had a fit at being left behind. His caution was not unwarranted, but the afternoon was bright and Ascerlon assured her they would be back before dark.

The transition in camps from followers to soldiers was pronounced. Enna had never felt so small. The men here were large and rough, head and shoulders taller than she was, and wrapped in steel. The white robes she and Trilaria wore shone like beacons even more than their pointed ears, and unwelcoming stares were directed their way. She could only imagine the difficultly they would have been in had the kindly mediturgeon not found them.

They entered a village, though it appeared that even the most peaceful of structures had now been entirely given over to the army. Unlike the bustling of the followers' camp, most of those here seemed to be exerting the minimum effort possible, whether men-at-arms by profession or one of the unfortunates pressed into service. More than a few were caring for armor and equipment that was dented and dinged. Ascerlon led them along what she assumed had been the main street to a farm on the outskirts.

"Here we are," Ascerlon said as they approached a barn. "Your order has taken residence here. My services are down a ways there, to keep the sick from the injured."

The smell of blood and unwashed bodies was strong as they entered, overpowering the lingering scent of animals and hay, and moans of pain filled the air. The cramped interior had been converted to a makeshift ward with the straw along both walls arranged into pallets. Not one was unoccupied. At least half a dozen women in the white robes of Elurithlia moved among the injured, rendering what aid they could.

"Sister Kayala?" Ascerlon called softly.

An older woman turned to face them, and her eyes widened in surprise as they fell upon the two elves. She moved quickly to greet them, beckoning another of the Sisters to join her as she walked by.

"We are always happy to see our Sisters," Kayala said. "Especially those come from so far away."

Enna returned her smile. "It is a relief to find you as well. We are here—"

"It's so gracious of you to help us in this dire time," the other woman said, her words smoothly inflected with an accent Enna had never heard.

She felt her annoyance rising at being cut off, but Kayala spoke before she could deliver a reprimand.

"Sister Marie is correct. Your aid is most welcome indeed. This is not the place to speak of your hardships. We have a tent nearby. If you would join us there, I would like to hear of your journey."

"A more private location would be appropriate," Trilaria

agreed.

Enna recognized the wisdom of it the moment the words were uttered, embarrassed that she had almost blurted out what was apparently a secret to these women. Why was the human world so tangled?

The four women left the barn, backtracking the way Enna and Trilaria had come for a short distance to a faded campaign tent pitched among several others in what might once have been a grazing field. Once they were all inside, Marie pulled the flap shut behind them and held it that way, keeping watch through the gap in the canvas.

"There are far too many untrustworthy ears in this camp," Kayala said without preamble.

"We had no idea that your purpose would need to be kept secret," Enna said. "Who else knows?"

"Including you, only the four of us. I dearly hoped that our meeting could have been held as it was supposed to, and I'm sorry that you had to risk yourselves in finding us."

"Nonsense," Trilaria said. "This war is not your fault."

"If you are under some threat, we can get you out," Enna said, already thinking of how. "Our Woodswardens could—"

"I'm afraid that we must remain here for now," Kayala said. "But that may be for the best. It is of necessity, not choice, that we find ourselves in this situation, and it is only by Her blessings that we have made it this far."

"I don't understand," Enna said.

"Someone has been trying to steal Shining Moon."

Enna glanced at Trilaria in alarm. From the corner of her eye, she saw Marie shudder at some dark memory.

"Who would do such a thing?"

"I don't know, but twice now they have nearly succeeded. We are strangers in this land and would not have reached here at all, were it not for those who walk the paths of Toush."

"We will help in any way possible," Trilaria said. "The protection of Alta Suralia is of paramount importance to us all."

"It is a relief to have someone to assist," Kayala admitted. "I have only a vague notion of where we are, but I am told that we are to return to Halisford after the fighting. My intent is to remain with them until then."

"That could be a long time," Enna cautioned.

"It might," Kayala agreed. "But it may allow us to elude our pursuers." She made a sweeping gesture that encompassed the entire camp. "There is so much suffering here, and many would have died without our intervention. I cannot help but believe that Eluria has placed us here for a reason."

Enna exchanged a glance with Trilaria. She had not expected Kayala to want to stay with this army, but there was little fault in her logic. Enna would not abandon Alta Suralia after finally reaching it, nor did it seem proper to demand Kayala hand it over under these circumstances. The weapon's return to Ildalarial would be a joyous celebration, and the old woman deserved to be the one to deliver it there.

"We came to escort you to Ildalarial and will not shirk from that duty," she promised. "Through whatever action we may, we will protect both you and Alta Suralia with our lives."

Kayala smiled sadly. "I pray that will not be necessary. We keep it hidden in this tent, though it remains unguarded far more than I would like. If you would be willing to aid us with the injured, we could take it in turns to stay close to it."

It seemed a workable plan, though not remotely what Enna wanted to do.

"It is your decision, as always," Trilaria said with one of her encouraging smiles.

"We will do anything to help," Enna said, praying it was the right answer.

* * *

Life fell into a pattern over the next few days. Enna and Trilaria helped Kayala and the other clerics from sunup to sundown, with only a few pauses in between. Some days were relatively quiet, while on others they were nearly buried beneath a deluge of wounded.

Listening to the soldiers she treated, a picture of the greater situation emerged, and it was not a good one. Enna had the sense that they were fortifying the general area, preparing for some large battle with the Ceringions. She found it difficult to believe that all the misery she had seen was due to simple raids and skirmishes, but, regardless of the reason, it was taking a toll on the soldiers.

Today had been particularly demoralizing. There had been a sortie of some sort that had ended badly, and dozens of men had arrived all at once. Enna had never been in the midst of a war before, and she wondered if they were always so miserable. Despite the misery surrounding them, it was oddly satisfying to care for so many people. It tested her endurance in ways she had never attempted, each restoration draining some of her own strength to affect the healing. She was working no harder than every other Sister here, but there was always a nagging guilt when it came time to rest and let another group of women take their place.

More exhausted than she had ever been, Enna returned with Trilaria to the small tent they shared. The quarters were cramped, and Enna was thankful that they had been able to retain some privacy, though their battered cots were not much more comfortable than sleeping on the ground.

"Should we try again tomorrow?" Trilaria asked.

Enna knew what she meant. They had each made attempts to get Kayala and Marie to abandon the army, but so far their efforts had yet to bear fruit.

"It won't hurt, but Kayala is set on her path."

"At least we're getting to meet lots of interesting people," Trilaria joked. "And the conversation is so stimulating."

Enna lay back and rubbed her face. "Most of them don't even bother to say thank you, although a few have given me coins."

"Me too. Maybe we can pay these Ceringions to leave before too long. I hear they love their money." Trilaria looked about conspiratorially and leaned close. "One of the almost-attractive ones asked me to marry him."

"Did you say yes?"

"Enna!" Trilaria exclaimed indignantly, though she couldn't hide her smile.

"You would make a fine farmer's wife," Enna teased. "With lots of little round-eared children to do the chores."

"You're just jealous," Trilaria shot back. "Anyway, he was a noble, doubtless a fair prince come to woo me away to his castle."

Enna rolled her eyes. "Even worse."

They both collapsed into laughter, giggling like little girls. Their levity was interrupted when Ilyand poked his head in the tent and waved them out. Groaning, they followed him into the night.

Instead of making for one of the many campfires lit to ward off the damp and the dark, he turned towards a shadowed stand of trees. Once they were sheltered within, he knelt beside a stout oak and beckoned them close.

"I will not mince words, Revered Sisters," Ilyand said, his voice low and insistent. "Every day that we wait increases the danger. We must take it. We cannot risk its loss again when the Actondel army falls."

"How do you know their defeat is imminent?" Enna demanded. "There are thousands of soldiers here."

"The Ceringions have thousands more, and they're better organized and better equipped. I've looked. The Kingdom forces have camped far too long in one location, and without suitable fortification. This army is ripe for destruction."

"It's also an army that barely tolerates our presence to begin with," Trilaria reminded him. "A word from Kayala, and they could send hundreds of men after us."

"They wouldn't. Not with the Ceringions beating them up so badly. It would be a small thing to retrieve Her weapon and slip away, this very night if you wish."

"How could we do that to Kayala?" Enna demanded. "She's been through so much already. We shouldn't be making enemies in a world already full of them."

"It's too risky," Trilaria agreed. "Better to keep helping them for now, and we'll try again to convince Kayala to flee. We cannot abandon them. If we can get her free of this mess, we can stay with her all the way to Fallhaven and allow events to play out as they should have from the start."

Ilyand looked to Enna once more, but she shook her head. "We cannot betray the trust of our Sisters."

"Your mother will be disappointed," Ilyand said as he brushed past her.

Trilaria offered her an encouraging smile. Her support was reassuring, but Ilyand's evaluation filled Enna with doubt. He was right about one thing: her mother would not at all be happy with the decisions she was making.

Those thoughts weighed heavy upon her throughout the night, allowing sleep to visit only in fits and spurts. The rising sun brought no relief, and even Trilaria's smile seemed forced as they made their way to the barn together. It would be foolish to ignore Ilyand's assessment, and she had to remember why they were here in the first place. This conflict between human kingdoms was not hers, and it was not Elurithlia's.

Ilyand was inconspicuously standing watch for them near the barn, and Enna motioned him closer.

"I did not wish to dismiss your concerns out of hand last night," she said. "If the camp is on the verge of being overrun, we will flee. But Kayala and Marie must come with us."

He began to protest but tensed suddenly as he caught sight of something over her shoulder.

Enna and Trilaria both jerked around, searching for the danger. Four armored men were moving purposefully towards them. Had their clandestine meeting the evening before been overheard? Ilyand's hand drifted towards his sword.

"No," Enna hissed at him.

The knight in the lead all but ignored the Woodswarden and Enna as he took Trilaria's hand in his own.

"My lady," the man said, bowing to brush his lips on her fingers. "I hope today finds you well."

"It does, good sir," Trilaria replied.

Enna relaxed, stifling a laugh at the attentions of Trilaria's 'prince.' If anyone tried to kiss *her* hand, she would slap some sense into them and deal with whatever trouble it caused. The knight seemed oblivious to her amusement, and Trilaria was too polite to reveal her thoughts.

"I informed Marshal Brouchard of your efforts on my behalf, and he requests your presence."

"I thank you," Trilaria said, gently withdrawing her hand, "but my actions have no more merit than those of any of our Sisters."

"You are overly modest," he said with a smile, "but then I'm a bit biased since I'm still alive. All who work here are appreciated, of course. Lest you think I intend to single you out, the invitation extends to your rangers as well. The Marshal has questions that he feels they would be exceedingly qualified to answer."

"Any way that we might help, of course," Trilaria said graciously. "If it would not be a slight, could Sister Enna remain here? There are so many in need."

Bless Trilaria for keeping her wits about her. It was a shrewd move, as it allowed at least one of them to remain close to Alta Suralia in case anything was to happen.

"No offense would be taken," the knight assured her.

Trilaria gave her an amused smile as she followed the knight away. Ilyand's look was more troubled as he and the other Woodswardens trailed behind. Enna couldn't think of any reason the commander of an army would want to talk to them right now, but she set her worries aside as she returned to the makeshift hospital.

Half the morning had gone by before the horns and drums began to rumble, signaling the start of another battle. Trilaria had yet to return, nor had there been any message from Ilyand. Their absence was becoming unsettling. Enna stepped outside to look for any sign of them. Kayala emerged right behind her, followed by three other clerics.

"Could you come with us today?" the old cleric asked. "This facility is overflowing, and many of the injuries could be treated closer to where they occurred."

"Of course."

It was impossible for Enna to refuse, despite her growing worry for Trilaria. Kayala was a giving woman who pushed herself more than she asked of others. If only her sense of self-preservation was as strong.

Enna followed the elder cleric to the edge of the town and across a field of trampled corn, coming to a stop much closer to where the army had formed up than felt comfortable. The sounds of battle were everywhere, but Enna was too short to see over the ranks of soldiers in front of her. There was absolutely nothing appealing about looking at the backs of hundreds of men standing in a field, and she prayed the wind would change so she wouldn't have to smell them either. It was a pleasant spring day, completely wasted on this pointless war. A wagon came skidding to a stop in front of them, a pair of wounded knights in the back.

Enna moved with the other Sisters to help, then froze as a flash of white caught her eye. On a short hill near the center of the formations, beneath a clustering of house banners, stood a group of knights, the Woodswardens, and Trilaria. Why was she so near the fighting?

Kayala had taken note as well. "I do pray she retreats soon. I dislike being even this close."

Enna's heart beat fast as worry threatened to consume her. She stood rooted in place, oblivious to the wounded before her. Why would Trilaria endanger herself for an army that could just as easily have been pointed at Ildalarial? She considered running to the hill with some excuse to retrieve her but could see no easy route through the throngs of soldiers marching here and there.

The sound and tempo of the conflict shifted suddenly, a change that caught everyone's attention. Enna knew nothing of warfare on this scale, but even she could tell that whatever had just happened was not good.

The activity on the hill turned frantic. The commanders took weapons in hand as the black-armored soldiers locked ranks. Horses bucked their riders, bolting in every direction. Ilyand was pulling Trilaria back. The other Woodswardens drew bows and began firing.

And then Enna saw it.

A large reptilian head dominated by a mouth filled with sharp teeth rose into view. Massive shoulders appeared next as the creature mounted the far side of the hill. Arms longer than a horse flailed about, its gleaming claws slick with the blood of its victims. It was a thing of legend and nightmares, an urtrifornu—a demon.

The hulking monstrosity tore through the defenders with unbelievable brutality, as if they were children with wooden toys. Arrows, spears, and swords failed to penetrate its thick hide. Trilaria shook off Ilyand's grip as she seized her symbol of Elurithlia and faced the massive creature. Flashes of silver lit the air as she invoked the might of her goddess, deflecting one and then another of the demon's attacks. But without any way to damage the creature, it only delayed the inevitable. First one and then another of the Woodswardens were trampled beneath the creature's hooves. Ilyand interposed himself at the last moment, but he was swept aside. The demon's claws ripped into Trilaria, tearing her open and flinging her in pieces to the ground.

Enna could only scream helplessly as she collapsed to her knees. The demon's victory roar trumpeted across the battlefield from atop a now lifeless hill. Finished with its decimation, the creature disappeared down the far side of the hill. Soldiers were rushing to reclaim it, but the most precious things upon that mound of dirt were already lost.

* * *

Enna woke with the sun, but there was no waking from the nightmare that haunted her. Trilaria was dead, her body and those of the Woodswardens consigned to the ground. Beneath the light of the moon, Kayala had said the prayers that needed to be said, bestowing the final blessings on their departing souls. The other Sisters had done their best to comfort her—far more, in fact, than she would ever have expected—but there was nothing that could fill the emptiness inside.

She returned to the hospital out of habit, her body going through the repetitions of the day before as her mind sought some way to change the past. She accepted the burdens of Trilaria's duties atop her own, a desperate effort to somehow replace what was gone. It would be her penance for all the mistakes that had brought them to here, but she had no idea what she might gain from serving it.

The moon chased the sun from the sky and reigned supreme until being vanquished once more by the dawn, but Enna barely noticed. Eventually, her hands began to tremble with every restoration, and fog crept into her mind.

She barely realized she was still in the barn until a gentle hand on her shoulder brought her fully to awareness.

"You should rest," Kayala said.

Enna licked her parched lips. "There is so much to do."

"And there will be just as much tomorrow. You must care for yourself if you wish to care for others, or you do them a disservice."

Enna recognized the wisdom of her words and allowed the old woman to steer her towards the exit. "Eat. Sleep. Seek the solace that only our Mistress may provide."

Enna promised that she would but felt Kayala's concerned gaze on her as she made her way from the barn. Too tired to sleep, she stumbled past her tent and drifted about the camp. There was no laughter or comradery, only somber expressions and muffled conversations. A few soldiers bragged of their martial deeds, others of their brushes with death. One man even made claims of being resurrected by an angel with eyes of blue, as if such a thing were possible. Sadness was everywhere, and it pushed her further into despair.

It was all her fault.

Had she listened to Ilyand, or been more forceful in her arguments with Kayala, none of this would have happened. It was the cruelest of fates to be spared the consequences of her own mistakes when Trilaria had paid so dearly for them.

Her resolve hardened, and she vowed that their deaths would not have been made in vain. Alta Suralia had to reach Ildalarial, and if Kayala could not be convinced to flee, Enna saw no other choice but to spirit away the hammer and carry it to Ildalarial herself. She would deal with whatever stain on her honor such an act would leave.

A voice called to her urgently, cutting through the gloom of her defeat, and she turned to the soldier now running towards her.

"My lady, please," the man said breathlessly. "We've a man wounded by spear yesterday who's not waking up."

"Show me," Enna said, shaking off her lethargy.

They hurried to a man who lay unmoving on the ground, and Enna knelt beside him. Her fingers went to his neck but found only the barest signs of an erratic heartbeat. She peeled away the makeshift bandage wrapped around his side, taking measure of the amount of blood that had escaped beneath it.

Looking up at his companions, she gave a small shake of her head. "I may ease his passing, but he is beyond any restorative arts."

They took the news stoically, likely aware of the verdict even before she had arrived. Enna allowed a moment in case they wished to deliver any final words, but when none were forthcoming, she recited the prayer for those leaving this life for the next, so tired that she forgot to say it in the human tongue. She gently closed the soldier's eyes as she concluded. "I am very sorry."

One of his companions offered a coin in payment, but she waved it aside. What good was money to her now? She stared at the ground, barely noticing as they carried the man's body away, and helplessness washed over her. No matter which of the paths before her she chose, it would only make things worse.

I am not a warrior, and I do not want to be a thief. Show me the way, Elurithlia, for I am lost.

She lifted her eyes to the sight of a young man wrapped in the layered greens and browns of a Silvalarian Woodswarden but with hair and eyes far darker than any of her distant kin. A cherished deer hoof knife at his side told of services rendered to her people while the sword on his opposite spoke of promises unfulfilled, but it was the compassion within the impossible depths of those eyes that tugged at her heart.

She grasped his outstretched hand, and he pulled her to her feet.

Any story of sufficient size and breadth requires that some details be sacrificed in the telling. To recount every footstep and emotion would require a lifetime to write and another to read. This particular scene was cut from *Hunter's Moon* not due to a lack of merit but simply because it was time for the story to move ahead. Tormjere and Kataria had been running across the kingdom for some time now, seeking the hoped-for protection of her uncle, and there was little to be gained from extending the journey.

And yet it always stuck with me.

I continued to recall these events as fact long after the book was published, even to the point of accidentally referencing it in *Weaponforger*. While not the most dramatic, it was a notable moment in Kataria's deepening relationship with her goddess, one which also provided a glimpse into the history of their ever-expanding world.

It takes place concurrently with the previous story, not long after their narrow escape from the ambush in the alleys of Bexville and just before their arrival at the conflict Enna was tragically mired in. It was a time when hunger and fear were their only travelling companions, and the comforts of Kataria's royal life were nothing but a distant memory...

Echoes of What Was

Kataria trudged wearily along the trail a few steps behind Tormjere, wondering for the thousandth time when it would all end. The afternoon was sunny and the forest around them pleasant, but the crossbow bolt that had nearly ended her life as they fled Bexville remained vivid in her memory even now, days later. It was the latest in a series of near calamities that seemed to prove that the entire world had turned against her. The near-abduction, the goblins, the river trolls, the constant pursuers—if she thought about it too long, she was certain she would simply collapse here in the middle of nowhere and cry.

All she wished for was to reach her uncle Brouchard and return to the safety and comfort that she had known as the Princess of Actondel. But that felt so far away now that she had begun to doubt such things could ever be reclaimed. What would she do if she could never return to who she was?

"Let's rest here," Tormjere said, pausing at a narrow stream cutting across their path.

Kataria knelt at the edge of the stream and bent her face

towards the water, more thankful for the pause than she cared to admit. Her symbol of Eluria swung freely as it dangled around her neck, but she caught the sacred disc before it dipped into the water. She drank straight from the stream as would any wild denizen of the forest, thirsty enough to not care in the least what it might look like.

Once satiated, she sat back on her heels and looked up through the trees at the blueness of the sky. The sun was bright and warm, but the lush canopy of the forest kept it cool and comfortable. It would have been so easy to lie down and close her eyes, but she stood instead, assuming the watch as Tormjere crouched to fill their waterskin and take a drink of his own.

They resumed their trek without words, a shared glance the only communication needed to know that both were ready. The random intrusion of their thoughts on those of the other had been as sparse today as their conversation, which was actually reassuring. There was little to be gained by listening to each other's thoughts, after all, and she still hoped that whatever had caused it would wear off soon.

Despite her best efforts to distract herself with the natural beauty around her, images of the men she had killed intruded roughly on her thoughts. Or that Tormjere had killed. They had worked together in fighting their way from that darkened alley in Bexville, making them equally complicit no matter which of them had struck the killing blow. Yet she could not deny the violence she had dealt. The wet crack of the man's head as she had struck him with her warhammer still set her teeth on edge, even as it mortified her for having done it.

She recoiled from those thoughts of death, trying desperately to turn to more pleasant memories, though there was no turning away from what she was becoming.

"There's something up ahead," Tormjere said, pulling her away from her dark thoughts.

There was more curiosity than caution in his voice, and so it was with interest that she followed his gaze through the tangled underbrush. His eyes were better than hers, and it took several more steps before she could identify the ruins of a stacked stone wall beneath the leaves and moss. She turned towards it, eager to have something different to focus on.

The row of stones intersected with another, giving the impression of a small octagonal building. Closer inspection revealed weathered, almost indecipherable symbols carved into some of the stones: shapes of trees and animals and birds and other natural things. Both the shape and the decorations were as different as they were intriguing.

"Looks elvish," Tormjere said, running his fingers over the stones.

None of the histories she had been taught made mention of elves living in the Kingdom, but she supposed anything was possible. This area had always been sparsely populated, a factor that was heavily influencing their difficulties in traversing the terrain.

There were other contours in the forest that, upon further inspection, appeared far too regular to be natural. It was difficult to decipher, like a picture drawn in the sand and then half washed away by the tide, but as they wandered among the outlines it was not long before the impression of streets and dwellings was revealed.

"Seems a good place to stop for the night," Tormjere said.

"These walls are tall enough to mask our fire, and there's still enough light for me to try and catch some dinner."

"Food would be nice," she agreed. A decent meal was a part of her life that had been sorely missing of late, along with so many things that she had taken for granted. It was depressing to wonder at how many would return and how many were gone forever.

Tormjere selected a clear spot within the squarish outline of what might once have been a house and dropped his pack.

"I won't be gone long," he said. He looked in every direction, probably committing their location to memory, then slipped into the woods.

Having insufficient skills to contribute to the hunt, Kataria made herself comfortable in a corner of the walls and waited. At least it gave her a chance to rest her tired feet. Her eyes wandered up and down the trunks of the trees, then drifted along the branches interwoven into the lush canopy, finally coming to rest on a break in the leaves that allowed the blue sky to show through. There was a neatness to the gap that suggested the work of a deliberate hand. She sought to dismiss it as the imaginings of a weary mind, but the thought remained stubbornly insistent no matter how many times she looked away.

Curious, she decided to investigate. Her sense of direction in the woods might have been getting better, but she placed Tormjere's pack atop the wall to mark her starting point, just to be safe, then made her way along a flattened trace that might once have been a road.

She had never visited an elvish town or even seen a realistic depiction in paintings, yet her imagination constructed shops and homes atop the ruined foundations and filled the street with laughter and motion. The echoes of conversation and song drifted enticingly through the nonexistent shutters, but her feet kept her moving unerringly through the tangled underbrush towards her destination. A pair of matching trees framed an opening, and she stepped between them into a clearing.

Unlike the heavy undergrowth she had just traversed, the ground here was level and the grass wild but not high. The circumference was so regular that it formed an almost perfect circle, and a shallow depression of similar shape was outlined by a raised ridge in the center of the clearing. It could have been idle fancy, but she thought of it as a small reflecting pool.

Without knowing why, she found her hand drawn to her symbol of Eluria. There was no shrine or alter, no statue to lend piety to the space, but there was significance here that transcended its physical dimensions. It pulled at her, drawing her forward.

She knelt at the edge of the depression, brushing away moss and grass to reveal a stone that was smoothed by more than nature. Faintly outlined upon the rock was a shape that was almost, but not quite, a half moon. It seemed either a minor error or an impressively precise depiction. Further investigation revealed another stone of uniform size beside it, this one bearing a symbol that was almost exactly the same. The difference between the two, if any, was nearly imperceptible. That gradual shift continued as she moved along the line, uncovering three more before finding one that was a perfect half circle. She sat back on her heels, amazed at the artistry. Then she glanced up.

Just above the treetops, in perfect alignment with her and the stone, hung the moon, half its surface blazing white as the opposite side lay in shadow.

They sat there for a time, each regarding the other. There was no rush of elation, no irrational fervor as she had experienced atop the mountain before. But there was something. It was… peaceful, calming. An assurance of what was to come. Dusk gathered and the forest darkened, yet she remained as she was, unwilling to relinquish the sensation until Tormjere's frightened shout broke the silence.

"I am here!" she called out as she stood. With a last, longing look at the moon, she hurried towards him.

Twilight had deepened the shadows to the point that she could not see him, but the memories of her imagined town remained somehow vivid enough to guide her back down the same road she had already walked.

"What were you doing?" Tormjere demanded when she returned.

"I was just looking at something," she replied. "There was not anything else to do."

He frowned at that explanation.

"Was your hunt successful?" she asked before he could question her further.

He held up a brace of rabbits in answer, then got to work dressing them. The fire was brought to life with his magic, and before long there was meat roasting. She barely paid his ability any mind, no matter how strange it was for a ranger to possess the talents of a sorcerer. There was no telling what fates had conspired to cross his path with hers, but it was the only thing that had gone right since she had left Merallin and that could not be a simple coincidence. Her eyes drifted back to the moon.

Thank you, Eluria.

Introduction to
"Return to Maetholmir"

The years between *Hunter's Moon* and *Weaponforger* occupy one of those lulls in the story that seems, on the surface at least, to be endlessly intriguing. There are so many challenges that arise in an isolated wilderness settlement, surrounded by goblins, wyverns, and other unwelcoming neighbors intent upon eating you.

Such a dangerous location doubtless led to a host of fascinating encounters for the inhabitants, yet their continuous struggle to provide shelter and sustenance becomes monotonous in the telling.

This is not to say that nothing of interest happened during that time, however. Many a noteworthy event and minor adventure did occur, several of which were hinted at upon Tormjere's return. Any number of these might be considered noteworthy by the scholars of our time, but there was one in particular which would have a lasting effect on Enna.

Many were the nights that she sat awake, staring up at the majesty of the Three Sisters and wondering what to do. Fate had been unkind to her since she left her home, forcing her to endure horrors that would have crushed the spirit of a less resilient soul. Worse, she found herself caught between the compelling pull of two worlds, neither of which aligned with where her heart was leading. As she always did during times of confusion, she turned to her goddess, seeking both direction and truth.

The answer to her prayers arrived when she needed it most, but the solution was not at all what she thought it would be.

Return to Maetholmir

Enna knelt at the edge of the cliff, waiting silently in the half light of the approaching dawn. The morning was cool, though summer had arrived nearly a month before, and mists shrouded the thickly forested slopes of the mountains in every direction. To her left, at the north end of the valley, the uniquely sharp points of the Three Sisters rose high above it all, standing in stark contrast to the smoothed peaks of the lesser mountains around them.

The day dawned as it always did in this uninhabited wilderness, quiet and still, a gentle transition from darkness to light, from the soft hum of insects to the stirring of birds. There were more birds here than she had ever beheld in the civilized lands of Actondel or even her forested home of Ildalarial, where nature and structure blended in harmony without one trying to dominate the other.

The wind held the promise of rain, a frequent occurrence this time of year, but it had not deterred her from greeting the morning as she often did, from this secret location along the valley's eastern rim. The sun touched this place hours before it would reach the clearing they used as their glade of worship on the island, and there was plenty of time for her to return for the morning prayer with Shalindra and Marie. It was strange to thank Elurithlia twice each morning for Her nightly vigil, but the fortunes of their settlement were steadily improving and so the extra appreciation felt warranted. It would have been dangerous to draw attention to herself by breaking the silence, so the words of her prayer passed straight from her heart to her goddess.

She chose not to linger when the prayer was done for the same reason, despite the beauty of the vista. Placing the rising sun at her back, she descended down into the valley, her quiet, unerring footsteps following the web of game trails leading back towards the village.

The eastern side of the valley was mostly clear of goblins, but that was in large part due to the benevolence of the rockhurlers. The strange stone beings were tolerant of their new human neighbors, an arrangement that was due exclusively to, of all people, Honarch. How the sorcerer had managed to win them over was beyond her understanding, and while he had been full of useful surprises like that, she still found it difficult to feel safe around him. The only reason for any level of trust was because he had been in this valley before, with Tormjere.

Her foot tripped over a root at the thought of him. He had disappeared as they fled the Kingdom, sacrificing himself to enable their escape. He had probably been captured, perhaps even killed. Neither fate was what he deserved. She had argued vehemently that they should go back and find him, but Shalindra had just as strongly refused. What Shalindra knew about his disappearance, and how she knew it, remained a mystery. She still refused to speak about it even now, but it was clear that she held out hope for his return. It was a touchy subject that Enna avoided whenever possible, no matter how many times she wished he was here.

Her eye was pulled towards an arrangement of sticks on the path in front of her, and she stopped short. It was no idle pile created by dried limbs as they fell from the trees above. The pattern clearly represented the elvish glyph for 'friend,' and it had not been there when she had passed this way an hour before. The spark of elation it triggered was quickly muted by the manner of its appearance.

"Revered Sister."

The voice was soft and calm enough to keep her from jumping, but not reassuring enough to keep her hand from grasping her symbol of Elurithlia. She sought the location of the voice, more than willing to invoke the protections of her goddess upon its owner. Not ten paces away, an elf in the layered greens and browns of a Woodswarden stepped from behind a tree.

"Are you well?" he asked.

"That remains to be seen," she replied warily, listening for other movement around her while her eyes darted back and forth. His dress and accent placed him from Ildalarial, but this valley was so far from those borders it might as well be on a different continent.

Her reticence seemed to unsettle him, and he shifted nervously. "The humans have placed no shackles on you, have they?" he asked. "If so, we can see to your safety."

"They have no hold over me, save friendship. If I'm not back soon they will come looking for me."

He relaxed a little. "We would never seek to delay you, Revered Sister."

"Then perhaps your friend can show himself." It was a guess, but Woodswardens rarely travelled alone.

He whistled the call of a robin, and within moments another elf in similar attire came jogging up the trail to join him. "Revered Sister," the newcomer said to her with a bow.

"This is Tirin, and I am Drayle," the first Woodswarden said. "I apologize for causing you any distress. I only wished to speak with you without the intrusion of human ears."

"They would be less of an intrusion than you might believe, but you are still blocking my path."

Drayle dipped his head in apology, and both Woodswardens stepped to the side. "Your safety is of our highest priority, Revered Sister. Please allow me to explain our purpose here. We have escorted a delegation of your Sisters through the wilderness to this sacred valley."

Despite her initial caution, Enna's heart leapt at the possibility of being among her people once more, especially here.

"I pray that the wilderness was kinder to your journey than it was to mine," Enna said. "Where are they?"

"Not far to the south. We came ahead to ensure that we would not be met with any… misunderstandings."

"Unless your intentions are hostile, there is nothing you or they need fear from our settlement," she assured him.

"What of the goblins?" Drayle pressed, though he appeared relieved. "I confess that we were surprised to see you walking in these woods alone."

"The rockhurlers keep this part of the valley free of goblins."

Drayle's eyebrows shot up in surprise. "The stone wardens are real? You've seen them?"

"Many legends of this place are true. We have done the rockhurlers some favors, and, as the goblins of this valley are our mutual enemies, they see fit to protect us." It was an exaggeration, as Honarch was the only one they had ever defended, but it was close enough.

"Fascinating," Drayle said. "Such information will be gladly received."

"When will my Sisters arrive?" Enna asked, hoping it would be today.

"Look for our arrival two days hence. We will approach from below the falls, where the lake drains into the river."

"You should keep to this side of the waterway," Enna cautioned. "The ancient road that once carried our pilgrims along the western bank is under the control of the goblins."

Drayle bowed. "Thank you for that, Revered Sister. Shall we escort you back to your camp?"

She had been so long removed from the courtesies given to those who wore the white of Elurithlia that her ire rose at the implication that she could not take care of herself, but she managed to keep most of the annoyance from her voice. "I'll be fine."

"Then we will return soon. Farewell."

The two Woodswardens departed, melting into the woods so quietly that not a single leaf moved to mark their passing.

Enna raced towards the village, eager to tell Shalindra the news. After so long alone, she was certain that this visit would bring the help they so desperately needed.

* * *

The elves arrived in the early afternoon two days later, exactly as Drayle had promised. The sun shone bright in a cloudless summer sky, though the air remained cool this close to the lake. Enna stood waiting for them with Shalindra, Edward, and a handful of self-important people who styled themselves as dignitaries. A fair number of villagers had joined them in the common pasture that served as a communal gathering place, not because elves were arriving but simply because *anyone* was arriving at all.

Enna looked around the random distribution of houses and shops that would present the first impression of this nascent settlement. The buildings were rough and utilitarian, lacking embellishments or artistry. An imperfect wall of modest height ringed the village proper, the sharpened logs that composed it covered with the scratches and scars of multiple assaults. It was an altogether poor display, though it felt absolutely palatial compared to the virgin forest that had greeted their arrival. Enna fidgeted as she wondered what her Sisters would think of it all.

"I cannot wait either," Shalindra said, mistaking her nervousness for excitement.

The sound of approaching horses prevented Enna's response.

The elves filed towards them all on foot, which was not unusual for a race who preferred walking over riding but was definitely a surprise given how far they had travelled. Birion had ridden out that morning with a small squad to guide them in. The former knight, ever astute at diplomacy, had chosen to give up his mount and walk with them in a sign of friendship, but even without his horse he towered head and shoulders above them. Not for the first time, Enna considered how fortunate they were to have such a man with them.

Most of the elves were dressed in muted earth tones, as they typically wore when travelling. The three women in front, however, each wore sleeveless white robes that matched Enna's own, though theirs were in much better condition. It was a symbolic number, given the history of this valley and the trio of mountains that rose above it. There was something familiar about the oldest of the three, but Enna struggled to place her. The woman's flaxen hair was woven into a long braid held tight by rings of silver, and she moved with grace and poise completely out of place from those around her.

The woman's eyes sought hers, and beneath that questioning gaze Enna felt her breath catch in her throat. This was no simple member of her order; it was Amalira, one of the most senior members of the temple who not only guided the faithful but also held a position on the ruling Grand Calontier—or at least she had the last time Enna had been in Eitholmir.

After so many years away from her people, it hardly mattered to Enna. It could have been a gaggle of initiates in their first robes shuffling in, and she would have been just as happy to see them.

Edward, as the appointed lord of the valley, stepped forward to greet them. "Welcome to Newlmir."

Enna waited for the newcomers' reaction to the mangled name that had been assigned to the settlement. It was a bastardization of New Something-or-other, where many of these people had come from, and Maetholmir, the ancient elvish name of both this valley and the city which had once resided here. She had struggled not to vomit when they had decided upon that name, but there were so many more important issues to tackle at the time that it had not been worth further debate.

Amalira smiled brightly, regardless of what her opinion of it might have been. "Your welcome is most appreciated," she said, her voice carrying the accented inflections of someone less familiar with the human tongue.

"I am Edward Deurmark, Commander of our town. Please allow me to present my cousin, Shalindra."

"We've heard so many tales about you," Amalira said. "It is good to see Elurithlia represented so prominently here."

"Thank you," Shalindra replied. "Enna works harder than I to make it so."

Amalira's smile grew warmer as she stepped forward to embrace her. "Ennathalerial, it is good to find you well after all these years."

"As it brings joy to my heart to see you once more," Enna said. "We are honored that you would make such a journey."

Amalira's eyes went towards the Three Sisters. "To stand here in this place that is so sacred to us all, no cost is too great."

In that, Enna did not doubt her sentiments. She remembered her own elation the first time she beheld the pillars from which Elurithlia had been raised to the heavens, and she would have questioned the devotion of any Sister not affected by the sight of those three jagged peaks rising so high above the others.

"Hopefully it is a price that we can lessen over time," Shalindra said. "You must be tired after your journey. Our luxuries are few, but we have prepared what I pray are suitable accommodations. Would you like to see them?"

"The day is young, and it is invigorating to be standing in this place," Amalira replied. "Could we visit your temple first and give our thanks?"

"Of course," Shalindra said. "I will show you the way."

"I'll see to quarters for your men," Edward added.

Amalira accepted the offer with a gracious nod and then turned to Shalindra. "We were amazed to learn that even part of this valley was being reclaimed, and I immediately volunteered to come and see for myself."

"I am certain that was an arduous undertaking," Shalindra said, "but I am thankful that our small efforts enabled it."

Shalindra directed the elves towards the island while Edward signaled for the men and horses and— Actually, Enna realized, the elves had arrived without even pack horses. That was odd, but she shrugged it off as she fell in with the two Sisters behind Shalindra and Amalira. Both women smiled at her kindly, but their attention was on Shalindra as she pointed out different parts of the village.

Enna was almost giddy to be around her people, and a multitude of questions about her homeland threatened to spill out. She swallowed them with effort, resolving to wait for a more private time for that conversation.

"Our first night, we slept here on the open ground," Shalindra was telling them, gesturing to the lake shore.

Enna remembered it as a terrifying time. They had stopped here out of necessity, exhausted after their harrowing flight through the wilderness. Luck had been with them, however, as the lake's shoreline was gently sloped enough to allow fishing with nets and the ground flat enough to be worked. The sizable lake had yet to be given a consistent name, and Enna remained unable to recall its prior elvish label. She would have to see if Amalira remembered.

"We found the ground fertile…" Shalindra's explanation continued.

The ground *was* rich, and crops had begun to take hold from the day they were planted, though the harvest remained well short of what was needed to feed everyone. As the structures had gone up, the striations of society had begun to take shape. The more industrious families were already increasing their wealth and comfort, while the lazy were spending their time working for those who worked harder.

The women walked single file across the wobbly construction of floating logs which had been tied together to link the mainland with the island in the middle of the lake. Not far away, the beginnings of a stone causeway reached partway across. Workers labored with mortar and stone within a cofferdam to raise the next footing, but it was to where the span itself was being built that the elves' attention turned. The bridge seemed to be lengthening of its own accord like sausage extruded into form. The rumbling sound of a slow-moving rockslide filled the air as the stone was pushed slowly towards the next footing by two tall, bulky figures of jumbled rocks. Honarch, the former Conclave wizard, stood a few paces behind the humanoid creatures, directing their work while also keeping an eye out for anyone who might wander too close.

The elves stopped to gawk.

"The rockhurlers have been a blessing," Shalindra said. "They are capable of fashioning simple shapes from solid stone like a sculptor would work clay, but they are deathly afraid of water, and so the footings have to be built by hand and raised well above the surface before they will shape the next span. We post guards to ensure that no one spooks them while they work, as they can react unpredictably when frightened."

"It's incredible," Amalira said. "How did you bend them to your will?"

"They are not beasts of burden," Shalindra corrected her.

"Honarch was able to reach some kind of understanding with them, though I cannot do justice in describing how."

That had been an incredible day. The refugees had been confronted by the stone creatures almost the moment they first struggled their way into this valley. Enna was certain battle would be joined, but Honarch had spoken to them through his magic. It had been a lengthy but fruitful exchange, eventually gaining their tolerance. Even now, he was the only one afforded their trust, though he seemed baffled by their willingness to help.

"The temple is barely begun…," Shalindra continued as they set foot on the island and turned north towards the "upstream" point of the generally triangular landmass.

It was a bit of an understatement.

What would one day grow to be the temple of Elurithlia was now little more than a clearing in the trees with cut stones positioned to mark where the walls would be. Amalira made polite comments as she viewed the garden—Enna's contribution to the construction effort—which was already beginning to show promise.

"It is not grand yet," Shalindra said, indicating the empty clearing, "but it is filled with Her presence."

"Elurithlia watches us from the skies above," Amalira said. "We have no need of material constructs to speak to her, which we must now do. If we may have a moment to give thanks for our successful journey?"

"Of course," Shalindra said.

The three elves knelt, aligning themselves with the trio of mountains at the north end of the valley. Silence settled over the clearing, with the trees still thick enough to block every external sound save the distant rumble of the waterfall.

Enna allowed herself a moment of quiet reflection as they prayed. It was almost surreal seeing elves here. She had not spoken to one of her kin since… since the day Trilaria died. Had it really been so long? Sadness welled up within her suddenly.

The gentle touch on her arm returned her to the present. Shalindra was watching her with concern, and Enna forced a smile as the elves completed their prayer.

"This place was well chosen," the elvish priestess said as she stood. "What guided you in its selection?"

Shalindra shrugged. "It felt right."

Amalira again seemed surprised, but Enna was not. If only her fellow Sisters could have seen the countless choices Shalindra made based on nothing but her feelings, and how they had always proven right in the end. But they were here now, and Enna would finally have someone with whom to share the joy Shalindra brought to the world.

* * *

It took all of a day and half before the novelty of the visit had worn off and people returned to their lives. While the village had yet to see its first merchant and even the simplest of elvish trinkets were eagerly bartered for, Amalira's group had little in the way of goods to trade. Even the news they brought was uninteresting to most, containing only the vaguest generalities of the goings on outside elvish borders.

Enna pondered this situation as she tended to the gardens that would one day flourish in front of the temple. None of this was a surprise to her, as most elves took no interest in the affairs of Actondel beyond those that immediately impacted their own borders. Their purpose in coming here had nothing to do with information or turning a profit. It was a religious pilgrimage, and that was all.

But it was more than that to Enna.

The customs of the elves were her own, their mannerisms and sayings ones she had repeated her entire life, and yet they felt different. Maybe it was the aloofness. Though friendly, they kept to themselves as much as possible. The Woodswardens were rarely present, likely taking the opportunity to investigate the parts of the valley that had not seen the tread of an elvish foot in centuries. There was nothing about any of it that was out of the ordinary, but there was wrongness all the same.

It was probably just due to her own stress and the passage of time, she thought. The almost two years since leaving Ildalarial had been anything but pleasant, and Shalindra had been a beacon of hope that she had eagerly clung to. It was only natural for Enna to have adapted to the world she was immersed in, so perhaps these changes within herself were simply being made visible now through the lens of her elvish Sisters.

Enna sat back on her heels, no less confused than when she had begun that line of thought. Amalira would be the ideal person to provide the guidance she needed, but she had yet to find a suitable time to speak to her alone. Today, Enna had a mind to change that.

She stood, looking around. One of the elvish Sisters, Kristala, was deep in conversation with Marie at the far end of the garden, much as she had been since the morning prayer. Enna had last seen Amalira walking with Shalindra, but now it was Sister Gemen speaking with Shalindra, and Amalira was nowhere to be seen. Enna frowned. The elves had been spending all their time with

Shalindra and Marie, but they were practically avoiding her.

She brushed aside any feelings of jealousy. They knew nothing of the humans in this valley, and so it stood to reason that they would be most interested in them. This was the perfect opportunity for her to speak to Amalira. She began her search for the senior cleric, smiling to Shalindra and Gemen as she walked past them.

"Do you think more of your people will visit us?" Shalindra was asking.

"I don't see why not," Gemen said. "It was once a common pilgrimage, even for those who followed other gods."

"What happened to end it?"

"Our histories blame everything from goblins to humans." She shrugged. "We really don't know. It's surprising that the loss was not better recorded."

It was a kindly mistruth. Enna had read those same histories, and more than one placed the blame squarely on the tide of human expansion across the continent.

Enna crossed the bridge to the mainland, hoping to find Amalira at the inn. Argus' grand enterprise, though still incomplete, was the only place in town large enough to house their guests.

As she entered, Enna saw that every table and bench had been removed and the floor covered with makeshift sleeping palettes. It was embarrassing that this was the best they could offer such distinguished visitors.

Argus limped around the counter to greet her. "Lady Enna, how are you this morning?"

"I'm well, thank you." She answered with a smile. "I'm looking for Sister Amalira.”

Argus shook his head. “Haven’t seen her since she left, but she usually doesn’t return until night. I would’ve assumed she was with you.”

Enna could have assumed that as well. She was about to thank him and continue her search, but he motioned her close. Glancing around to ensure they would not be overheard, he said: “Any idea how long your friends will stay?”

“I have no idea. Why?”

“My regulars aren’t coming in, what with us turning the place into a barracks. I tried setting some tables out back but it’s not the same. The elves are a nice enough sort, don’t get me wrong, but they’re bad for business.”

“I see your point,” she said. “When I find Amalira, I’ll ask.”

She thanked him for his time and returned to her search, wondering where the elvish priestess could be. The village was small, and she was running out of places to look. The only place she had not investigated was outside the stockade.

Just for the sake of thoroughness, she checked with the guards at the gate. The gate was open as it always was during the day, and two of Edward’s men stood guard. Both bowed politely as she approached.

“Has Sister Amalira passed this way?” she asked.

“Is she an elf?” the senior man asked. “One of them went for a walk outside again as she does every couple of days. I’m sorry my lady, I don’t know her name.”

“That’s quite alright. Was anyone with her?”

“No, my lady. She went alone.”

That was odd. Amalira was far too important a person to be

wandering the woods alone, elf or not. She briefly considered asking one of the guards to accompany her but decided it might project the wrong image and would certainly interfere with the conversation she wished to have. Thanking the men, she set off in the general direction they had pointed.

Her feet found familiar patches of stone and dirt out of habit as she crisscrossed her way along the trails, avoiding the leaves and twigs that would alert anyone to her passage.

Eventually, a patch of white amidst the lush greenness ahead caught her eye, and she altered course towards it. She began to call out a greeting but pulled up short as another elf materialized from the forest and reached Amalira first.

"Revered Sister," Drayle said to Amalira, coming to stand before the priestess.

Enna ducked behind a tree. A warm flush of guilt washed over her to be eavesdropping, but there was something about the Woodswarden's manner that felt wrong.

"What did you discover?" Amalira asked.

Drayle's voice became muffled, likely because he was facing away from her, and Enna strained to hear his answer.

"… at least two goblin tribes … side of the valley … near the waterfall, both burned to the ground … is clear, as was claimed."

"Did you locate Maetholmir or its sister city?"

"Regretfully not, Revered Sister … legends are to be believed, it was…"

Enna nearly stepped from behind the tree to join the conversation, though she could guess at what he was saying now. Maetholmir was not a city fashioned of stone and glass. It was said to have been grown entirely from living trees, an ancient and beautiful art which was now as lost as the location of the original city.

"The human defenses?" Amalira asked.

"... be overpowered, but ..."

Drayle's voice grew faint, but the implication that he had been evaluating the village fortifications and manpower was troubling. Why would they care about such things, unless their intentions were hostile? And if so, there was no way that only twenty elves could overpower a settlement of several hundred humans. Not unless there were far more elves hidden nearby.

Drayle asked a question that Enna could not make out.

"No more than three days," Amalira answered. "This is taking too long, and I do not intend to return empty handed."

Enna's blood ran cold. There was nothing in this meager settlement that anyone would want. Nothing, that is, except for Shining Moon. Word must have reached Ildalarial that Elurithlia's weapon was here, and now it seemed that they, meaning Enna's mother, had finally sent someone to retrieve it.

The secret meeting sounded as if it was winding down, and Enna hurriedly tiptoed away. When sufficient distance and trees were between them, she sprinted back to the village. She slowed her pace once inside the protective walls, but only enough to catch her breath as she pondered what to do.

The fragments of what she had heard were not specific enough to trouble Shalindra. Truthfully, she could fill in the missing parts of that conversation with words which would have rendered it far less threatening, but they did not feel right. She needed to tell someone, just in case. For that, she could trust no one but Birion.

She found him easily enough, training soldiers as he usually did in a small field on the island where a castle would one day stand.

"Lady Enna," Birion greeted her with a small bow. "You seem tense."

Enna started to speak then stopped, hating herself for what she was about to say.

Birion took note of her indecision and steered her away from any listening ears. "This visit from your countrymen has you worried."

"Yes," she replied softly. "This place is sacred to my people, as is the weapon that Shalindra carries. The convergence of the two might arouse passions that could lead to… misunderstandings."

Birion stroked his moustache. "I understand, at least enough to recognize what you're telling me. I'll double the watch while they're here and make sure Shalindra is never alone."

"Thank you," Enna said, breathing a sigh of relief.

It was all that she could ask of him. There was nothing to be gained from searching for the additional elves she suspected were hiding in the valley. The forest here grew thick, and Edward and Birion simply did not have the manpower to perform an effective search of so large an area. It was disturbing to be so suspicious of her kin, but she consoled herself with the knowledge that they had not been entirely forthcoming with her either.

Either way, she prayed that the remainder of their visit would remain free of strife.

* * *

"Enna! Enna!"

The panicked plea startled her awake faster than the heavy pounding on her door. Enna bolted out of bed, hastily pulling on a robe as she stumbled through the darkness of her cottage. Her fingers were already wrapped tightly around her symbol of Elurithlia by the time she flung open the door, revealing a panting soldier named Jace.

"What's happened?" she asked in alarm.

"It's happening!" Jace said, gasping for air. "Hurry."

He was already pulling her outside as she struggled to guess what he meant. Had there been an attack? And was it goblins or elves?

"Tell me what's wrong," she demanded, jerking her arm free. "And where is Shalindra?"

That brought him up short. "Ah… I don't know. Should I go and get her? It's Harriett. Her baby's come early."

Enna could've throttled the man right there in the street for frightening her so badly, but she settled for shoving him to the side. "Why didn't you say so to begin with?"

Fully awake now, she dashed across the bridge to the mainland and raced through the darkened streets towards Harriett's house.

The small dwelling at the edge of the water was lit inside and out, and Harriett's husband, Adney, was waiting anxiously outside the door.

"Hurry!" he called.

Enna slowed and raised a calming hand. She could already hear the sounds of the woman's labor, but the mother was not the only person that needed to be attended to at times such as this. "You did well to wake me. All will be well, in Her light."

She forced herself to project calm as she entered the single-room house. Harriett lay in bed, her hands twisting the bedsheets tight and sweat glistening on her brow as she strained under the direction of the midwife. Harriett's daughter had the fire stoked high, keeping the room warm as she watched nervously from the side. Enna gave the young girl a reassuring hug before taking station protectively at Harriett's shoulder. The midwife, a stout woman named Beatrice, looked up and gave her a reassuring glance before returning to her duties. Enna took that as a good sign but still said a quick prayer for both mother and child, hoping that she would not be required to save any lives tonight. The baby's head was already appearing, and Harriett was a strong and healthy woman, but there were never any guarantees.

The door flew open suddenly, and two women in hasty dress burst into the cottage. Enna recognized them both but could put a name to neither. They rushed to Harriett's side, each taking one of her hands in their own, and began offering encouragement to the struggling mother. The baby seemed in no mood to wait, and soon the newborn's cries filled the house.

Harriett collapsed back, exhausted, as the child was swaddled and brought to her breast. There were tears and joyful words as the women fussed over them both.

Enna felt a touch on her arm, and Beatrice leaned close. "If you could tidy up a bit, dear." The request was unworried but purposeful.

Circling around to where the midwife had been working, Enna placed her hand low on Harriett's abdomen and intoned a prayer of healing, channeling Elurithlia's glory into the mother and repairing the damage done from the birth. Harriett's breathing slowed as her pain eased, and she smiled up at Enna in thanks.

Satisfied that mother and baby would be well tended by the other women, Enna slipped quietly from the home.

Harriett's husband waited nervously outside, now joined by

several of his friends.

"All is well with them both," she said to Adney. "Beatrice will let you know when everything is settled enough to enter."

Adney let out the great breath of air he had been holding, then hugged her in excitement. He stepped back almost immediately, clearing his throat at the impropriety. She smiled to let him know it was alright, then made her way home—at a more serene pace this time.

The night was almost gone when she arrived, and her door still ajar from her hurried exit. Sunlight blazed across the perpetually snow-capped peaks of the Three Sisters while the valley remained in shadow, and the hush of the morning was broken only by the continuous drone of the massive waterfall beneath those lofty peaks. Her prayer thanking Elurithlia for Her nightly vigil flowed without thought from her lips, this time giving added thanks for the healthy birth.

Amalira's voice came floating from behind to break her reverie: "They're beautiful, aren't they?"

"They are indeed," Enna said without turning, afraid that her displeasure at being interrupted would be evident upon her face. She needed to speak to Amalira, but did it have to be now?

"I never thought I would live to see them with my own eyes." Amalira rested a gentle hand on her shoulder. "Is everything well?"

Enna glanced down at the blood staining her robes and waved aside any concern. "A child just arrived. I have not had time to clean up."

Amalira dropped her arm but did not move away. "I haven't midwifed a birth in decades, but it is a joyous occasion."

"They're becoming more frequent of late," Enna said.

"Shalindra, Marie, and I take it in turns to safeguard the mothers."

Amalira reacted with surprise. "Shalindra still performs such duties?"

"There aren't a lot of options here. It will be years before any of our initiates will be capable of such duties, if ever."

"And she carries Alta Suralia with her?"

Enna came instantly on her guard. "It never leaves her side, nor should it."

Amalira seemed to ponder that for a moment. "It's good that she treats it with the respect it is due, but would you not agree that this is a dangerous place for such a relic to reside, and equally treacherous for you?"

"Danger has surrounded me since the day I left home. One place is no different than another."

"What of those who departed with you?"

The question was jarring in its directness but not delivered unkindly. Though Enna had buried that loss in the past, she acknowledged that no one in Ildalarial would have any idea of what had befallen them. A lump formed in her throat at the thought of Trilaria's parents wondering at their daughter's fate.

"They fell on a nameless hill in a nameless part of the Kingdom, and there they remain."

"I'm sorry."

Enna clamped her mouth shut as she struggled to hold back the surge of emotion that came flooding in, even after so long. Why was Amalira bringing this up now?

"You were there pursuing Alta Suralia?"

"Yes," Enna said, gathering her composure. "Sister Kayala's efforts to bring it to Fallhaven were met with disaster, and she found herself swept up in the war between Actondel and Ceringion. She was hiding within the army in the field when we finally caught up to her and could not be convinced to leave."

"A convenient excuse."

"An honest reason, I believe. She was certain they were being pursued, and we witnessed deliberate attacks against Elurithlia's temples throughout the war."

"But it is goblins and remoteness that threaten Her weapon now, not armies."

"Remoteness feels like a blessing, most days."

"This is not where it, nor you, belongs."

Frustration leaked into Enna's response. "Who are we to make demands upon it?" She already knew where this was headed and was far too tired to deal with it.

"Every contingency has been planned for, if necessary."

Enna could not have been given clearer confirmation that there was a contingent of elvish soldiers in the valley if she had asked directly. She remembered similarly covert plans in place when she had first left to escort Shining Moon home, and this time she made no effort to keep the disgust from her face. "We seem to enjoy the thought of being thieves, of late."

"For Alta Suralia, we would face anything."

"With it, Shalindra already has."

They stared at each other for long moments, and while neither moved, Enna could feel the conflict of those opposing sentiments pushing them apart.

Amalira was the first to break the silence. "We followed your signs into the mountains and feared the worst when they disappeared."

"I was a little busy trying to stay alive."

"Why, then, did you not turn her towards the sanctity of Ildalarial? Both you and the hammer would have been safe there."

"Oh, of course. It would have made far more sense to traverse an entire kingdom filled with *two* armies trying to kill us. I don't know why that thought never occurred."

"Your attitude is inappropriate. There was a great deal of turmoil when you failed to return, and we have been through our own trials to come and find you."

"I'm sure they were terrible."

Amalira bristled. "Do not mock me, I have—"

"Never faced a demon!" Enna almost screamed. "Never stood before a giant of muscle and hate with skin like stone. Never been splattered with the gore of its rampage or felt its claws penetrate your flesh." Her hand jerked involuntarily to her stomach at the memory. "Do not speak to me of your trials."

Amalira's face had gone almost as white as Enna's hair, but whether from shock at what she had been told or at the tone in which it was delivered was impossible to tell.

Enna's fists clenched, and her entire body shook as the words continued to flow. "Demons are real. I've waded through the bodies left from their assaults, desperate to save what lives I could. Only Shalindra was capable of standing before them, and she did so with nothing but her faith and Alta Suralia."

"How can you expect us to believe that anyone who has not Ascended, and a human at that, could employ the sacred weapon of the Guardians?" Amalira demanded. "It has always been one of our race to hold that honor."

"I don't need be lectured on history," Enna snapped. "You're welcome to try to take it from her, since you clearly think she doesn't deserve it. I'll enjoy watching *your* arm shrivel and fall off."

"Ennathalerial!"

"That's what happened to the last person who laid a hand on it." Other than Tormjere, but that was neither here nor there. "It doesn't matter what you want, and it doesn't matter what my mother planned. Shining Moon is not mine and it is not yours. It belongs to our goddess, and it is She who decides its use."

Amalira sucked in a deep breath. "In that, you are correct, and I forgive you your manners. You have been forced to endure unimaginable hardships during your time with the humans, and it must have required many sacrifices. It is unkind of me to argue against what I have not seen firsthand."

Enna attempted to calm herself as well. This woman was not her enemy, no matter how narrow and frustrating her views. "Though the rulers of Actondel may rightly be named our adversaries, not every human is without merit. These are good people here who are bothering no one."

"But Shalindra is one of those rulers of Actondel," Amalira countered. "You must understand the influence that has on perceptions."

Enna almost laughed, but the bitter taste in her mouth choked it off. "Her own father tried to have her killed, and it was his vassals who chased us from the Kingdom. She is no more a member of that family than I am queen of the goblin tribes surrounding us."

Amalira grew quiet as she stared at the mountains. When she at last spoke, her voice was calm. "What you have shared explains much, even as it leads to a host of far more difficult questions. Neither you nor Alta Suralia can remain here forever. A Guardian must Ascend, and that Ascension can take place nowhere but Ildalarial." Amalira turned to face her once more, and this time there was no recrimination in her question. "When will you return to us?"

"When She tells me it is time," Enna said. "I do not know why Elurithlia brought us here, but I cannot believe that it was without purpose."

Amalira allowed the sweep of her gaze to encompass the structures on both island and shore. "Do you find enjoyment from living in these primitive conditions?"

"I reside in one of the most holy places on this entire world; what is there to be ashamed of? Maybe the reestablishment of Maetholmir is our purpose."

"A worthy goal, but not the stuff of legends. The portents were clear and were seen by all. The time of the Guardian is upon us, and we should not seek to delay it."

Nor should it be rushed to fit your own selfish needs, Enna almost said, but her anger had already drained away. There was nothing that she could say that would change Amalira's opinion.

The older cleric waited for a response, but when Enna failed to provide one, she turned away. "If there is help we may provide, I am willing to listen."

Enna only nodded her acknowledgment as Amalira left her to her troubled thoughts.

* * *

Enna barely slept for the next three days, certain that the elves would attempt to steal Shining Moon. Shalindra was aware of her edginess but had attributed it to her sadness at Amalira's approaching departure. She had even offered that Enna was free to leave with them and was under no obligation to stay, so kind was she.

Enna never would have imagined it, but she was happy to see her elvish kin depart. Amalira's visit had certainly failed to accomplish what she wanted, and in the process had shattered Enna's dreams of Shalindra's triumphant entry to the elvish homeland. It was clear now that there were some, perhaps many, among her people who would never accept a human woman as Guardian, no matter what proof was offered. It filled her with sadness to admit that her mother would be included in that group.

Yet there was still opportunity to prepare, and she thanked Elurithlia for the warning. She would not hurry Shalindra south. She was more secure here in this valley than she would ever be in the elvish capital. It was time for Shalindra to be told some of the lore that elves never shared with outsiders, and to learn all that Enna could teach of how to control talents that, up until now, had been intrinsically developed.

Edward and Birion could keep Shalindra safe from goblins, and, by Her light, Enna would see her protected from those who should have been her most devoted friends.

Introduction to
"Enemy of My Enemy"

It can be difficult to know what to make of that mysterious order of sorcerers known as the Conclave of Imaretii. At first glance, their actions appear undeniably selfish and counter to everything that is good and decent, yet the motives that drove those choices remain shrouded in secrecy.

Their existence predates that of the Reginum they surreptitiously controlled, a cabal of mystics desperately seeking to salvage whatever they could from a civilization on the verge of collapse. In that effort they succeeded, perpetuating arcane knowledge and ancient lore that would otherwise have been lost to the ravages of time and warfare.

And yet, as decades dragged into centuries, the wizards toiling to prevent another apocalypse slowly fell victim to the same hubris and secrecy that had necessitated their creation, and in so doing became blind to the danger they welcomed into their innermost sanctums.

Well, most of them.

Philosophers will often recount how, when the fate of nations is perilously balanced on a knife's edge, it is the decisions of a brave few which tilt the outcome towards favor or ruin.

This, then, is one such example.

Enemy of My Enemy

Verelli skidded to a stop as he reached the end of the darkened tunnel, the rubbery feeling in his legs leaving him on the verge of collapse as his lungs greedily gulped in huge gasps of air. The dim amber glow of the guide stones along the floor, each of which had flared to life as he raced past, faded one by one as they slowly caught up to him, until only the pair to either side remained lit. He considered himself a fit man for his age, and in much better condition than many wizards far younger, but his heaving chest reminded him that it had been years since he had been forced to run so far. Then again, it had been even longer since his life had depended upon it.

He cast a worried glance over his shoulder into the inky darkness, wishing that the guide stones would have provided their light just a little longer. His ears strained, listening for any further sounds of pursuit, and it was only with great effort that he put that uncertain blackness at his back and reached towards the dim outline of the door.

The latch opened at his touch with a soft click, but he hesitated with his hand on the threshold. What awaited him outside could be every bit as terrifying as what he had run from. He quickly reviewed the sequence of spells that might prove effective against the most likely threats, gathering his strength as he arranged the proper words on the tip of his tongue. With a prayer to whatever gods might be listening, he cracked open the door.

Fresh, moist air rushed in to replace the dank and stagnant contents of the tunnel, carrying the smells of damp earth and leaves. The outside lay in shadow, allowing only a faint sliver of light to enter with it. Verelli held his breath as he listened.

"It's clear," called a man's voice, one that was tight with fear but sufficiently loud to be unconcerned that anything might be close enough to hear. At least it was human.

Verelli pushed the door fully open and stepped through, emerging into a narrow gully that widened as it descended off to his left. Bushes and plants were plentiful but trees sparse, and upon their higher branches were the first hints of autumn color. The terrain had the appearance of a completely natural feature created by rainwater as it carved its way along the path of least resistance, but it had been shaped specifically to shield the entrance to the tunnel he had just vacated—even the outer face of the door had been carefully crafted to match the appearance of the dirt embankment. Near the top of the hill stood a man dressed in the common garb of one whose livelihood came from working the land, though that impression was as false as the draw they stood in.

"You might've been safer staying in there," the man said, his eyes locked on something Verelli could not see.

Verelli hurried upwards to join the false farmer, steeling himself for every possibility of what he might see, and yet the hellish vista that confronted him still tore a gasp of dismay from his lips.

Tythir was dying.

Towering flames blazed from one end of the sprawling city to the other, choking the air with dark clouds of ash that blotted out the rising sun. Winged shapes swooped and dove through the twisting columns of smoke, hunting like birds above a shoal of fish in the bay. Infrequent flashes of light marked where magic was employed, but the strobing colors flickered and died like so many sputtering candles. The roar of the fire mixed with screams and shouts created an indecipherable cacophony of noise. Thousands of panicked residents, many still in their nightclothes, clogged roads and fields as they fled in every direction.

His eyes were drawn to the hexagonal arrangement of the six towers of Solor-Majalis that rose from the rocky hills above the southern end of the city. A moment of disorientation swept over him as the tallest of the Conclave's towers appeared on the point farthest from the city instead of closest, until he realized that the citadel had not been twisted about; rather, an entire section of the Grandmaster's tower was simply gone.

Motion atop that ruined pillar caught his eye, and he watched transfixed as the missing top was replaced by the silhouette of a gigantic demon. It spread its arms and wings wide, basking in the destruction around it, and even from this distance, miles away, the creature was so large that Verelli could make out details on every massive appendage. The demon flung something over the edge, and he was struck by the sickening realization that the tiny shape plummeting towards the earth was almost certainly human.

Verelli turned away as the great demon launched itself from its perch to join its brethren in laying waste to the city, unable to watch any longer. "Is everything prepared?"

The false farmer tore himself away from the calamity and began walking towards the farmhouse. "It's all as it should be. The safe house is—"

Verelli cut the man off. "I'm not going to the safe house."

"But the protocols…"

"The protocols never accounted for an event like this. Are there mounts ready?"

"We've horses saddled in the stable," the guard affirmed, glancing back in the direction of the tunnel. "Were you the only one?"

Verelli wasted no time with looking back, afraid that if he turned around, he would run back and try to help. The futility of such an attempt was easily calculated, but that did not make the decision any easier.

"There was no one else."

The finality in his own words brought him to a stop outside the stable. He had to check one more time. Pulling his dohedron from a pocket, he tapped a query across the jeweled facets. The series of flashes would be replicated in Grandmaster Fellaxus' dohedron, *if* either device or owner still existed.

Receiving no response, Verelli adjusted the phase crystal and tried again, hoping that Erridan was free of the fighting. But again the device lay dark in his hand. His next message to Stellara went similarly unanswered. He repeated the exercise half a dozen times, but the only flickers of light came from his own efforts. Dismayed, he returned it to his pocket and pulled himself onto the closest horse.

"This location will not be safe an hour from now," he said to the guard. "Tell anyone who arrives to make a run for Avalta, and do the same yourself, when you must."

* * *

The smell of smoke still permeated Verelli's senses as he galloped into Avalta that same afternoon, though the miles-wide, sooty smudge polluting the eastern sky behind him was too far away to supply the odor. He had raced past half a dozen smaller towns as he charged along the road paralleling the Haliestos River, stopping only once to change horses at another Conclave "farm" roughly halfway between the two large cities. Judging from the bustling activity everywhere he looked, news of the calamity had yet to arrive. That would all change when the demons spread here.

Avalta, like most Ceringion cities, had taken down its battlements so many years ago that their remnants were almost impossible to find. The low walls of the original fortress still stood atop an escarpment rising from the middle of the city, but only a handful of gatehouses hidden somewhere within the sprawl of buildings marked the more formidable defenses that had once safeguarded the populace. He noted that the church of Amalthee appeared unusually fortified, with a contingent of armored men draped in ceremonial sashes of blue stationed around the perimeter, but beyond that, the city was wide open.

Multiple towers rose above the skyline, each the domain of a master sorcerer, but it was to a pleasant villa halfway up the hill beneath the fort that Verelli rode.

There was no tower jutting up from the compound, belying the fact that the most powerful wizard in the city lived here. Servants appeared and took his horse before showing him through

158

the arched gateway.

The villa was of traditional Ceringion architecture, with a continuous building of two story's height surrounding an inner courtyard, and whitewashed walls protected by the fired clay tiles of the roof. It was beside a central fountain within the courtyard that the servants left him as they went in search of their master.

Verelli paced impatiently as he waited, trying to think of the best way to break the news. Feston arrived on his own time, strolling languidly into the courtyard.

"Master Verelli, to what do I owe this surprise?" The question was polite but guarded, which was hardly surprising. The pair rarely saw eye to eye on the running of the Conclave, and their most recent debate had bordered on the uncivil.

"We have a breach," Verelli said, settling on the direct approach. "I believe there is an unattenuated portal inside Solor-Majalis."

Feston looked puzzled. "A breach? We've seen those before, and they are normally contained without excessive difficulty. I'm curious why you would feel the need to come all this way to tell me in person."

"It's no small disruption. Hundreds of demons came through."

Feston's eyebrows shot up. "That's different."

"You've received no word on this?"

"None, which is either cause for great concern or reason for me to doubt the veracity of your claims."

"I wish it was the latter. I fought my way free and fled through the tunnels before racing here." Verelli's shoulders slumped. "There wasn't anyone else to come with me."

Feston gave him a hard look, then pulled a dohedron from his pocket. His fingers danced across the jeweled facets in a series of practiced motions, which garnered no response. He made an adjustment before tapping out a shorter missive, but again there was no answer.

When the device remained dark after two more attempts, he looked back at Verelli. "I doubt that you've subverted everyone for some scheme, so I will take you at your word for now. How bad is it?"

"Our citadel is lost, and the city was being ravaged by fire and demon. I honestly don't know what's left."

"Nothing could be evacuated?"

Verelli shook his head. "If I hadn't been below the citadel and so close to the bolt hole, I doubt I would have made it out."

Feston paled. "The Grandmaster?"

"Likely gone as well. The top third of his tower was destroyed."

Feston motioned Verelli to a bench as he sat heavily. "How could this have been allowed? The controls around such magics are well defined."

"At first, I assumed it was simply an errant summoning. I was down in the basements doing some combustive research with Ravarro when we heard some disruption above, and the entire tower shook. We stopped the experiment and rushed towards the surface but were stymied before reaching there. The first demon we encountered was small but still difficult for the two of us to banish. We collected Montus as we worked our way up, and with him the next demon was easier to deal with." He shook his head. "Then we were confronted by strange centipede-like creatures that seemed to burrow through the rock. We tried to push through, but Montus and Ravarro were both killed in the attempt. With the way blocked, I fled through the tunnels."

"Once free, you did not go back?"

Verelli closed his eyes, but the memory was still sharp in his mind. "There was nothing left to save."

"You will forgive me if I decide to try," Feston said, fingering the summoning focus which hung around his neck.

"I would expect nothing less of you," Verelli replied, forcing a smile. "My opinions could be skewed by the shock of the attack, but I think that any rescue effort will have to wait until we have a solid understanding of what we face. First, we must focus on containment."

"It's a sound beginning, and I do not mean to question your judgement in the moment, but containing this will take significant resources. What you describe is as grand in scale as it is unprecedented. Let us assume that we are, indeed, dealing with a single unattenuated portal. It should be easy to close once found."

"That would be my hope, but where? It's probable for it to be located within Solor-Majalis, quite possibly in the Grandmaster's tower, but I saw nothing of the city except from a distance. This is frustrating to be debating events when we have so little to go on."

"Our network has been very quiet," Feston said. "With time comes clarity, and I agree that we do not need to be rash." He paused to consider something. "What do you intend now?"

Verelli had already plotted their next steps even as he had raced here. "Recent history has shown us that the combination of manpower and magic is effective against them. We will need to have the armies returning from the aborted campaign in Actondel gathered and repurposed."

"That could take months, and winter is approaching," Feston

pointed out. "This region has not existed without Tythir's stores since the great crop collapse some four centuries ago. If the damage is as extensive as you've described, it will put a strain on things and make many of the lords more recalcitrant. Most will seek to preserve what they have at the expense of their rivals. I'm sure the plots have already begun."

"I don't intend to wait on all of them," Verelli said. "Our losses will continue to mount with every passing day. There must be a push to retake Tythir before it gets completely out of hand."

Feston looked troubled. "Given that no one has been able to make contact with any senior member of the Conclave besides yourself, we may need to invoke the survivor's protocol."

Verelli had considered that eventuality as well, but he continued to hold out hope that more of his peers had survived. "The circumstances are dire, but to enact it now might further destabilize the situation."

Feston frowned at him reproachfully. "The protocol—which you are so fond of and helped develop, I believe—is quite specific in this matter."

"I know the protocols," Verelli snapped. "We must act, and we have precious few resources at hand. There is an open gate to the abyss of the demon realm a day's ride from here. Everything within sight of Tythir might be lost by nightfall. Within days, half this kingdom could be engulfed."

"Which is precisely why you must not stay here," Feston insisted, holding his ground. "Nor can you charge back into the fray. Our leadership is gutted. Probably three quarters of our members were in the city, and they may all be lost. Without a governing body, those of us left will be less of a Conclave and more an uncoordinated mob."

Verelli rubbed at his temples as the words sank in, then slumped in resignation. "Though I do not want to admit it, you are correct. My first responsibility must be to the survival and restoration of our Conclave."

"If it's any consolation, it means that you are entitled to order me around now, at least until this crisis ends."

Verelli could not help but chuckle. "My most worthy sparring partner now at my beck and call. There is a silver lining to be found."

"Mind you, I'll admit to none of it," Feston said with a laugh, then turned serious once more. "We've had our disagreements, a few of them rather loud, but I like to think they were more professional than personal. Whatever needs to be done to preserve our Conclave, I shall do."

"Thank you. That is my intent as well. You still maintain a strong connection to the Tyrati of this city?"

Feston nodded.

"I would suggest that he begin to fortify his city and see to the safety of our members as we regroup here."

"He's probably cowering beneath his bed, if he even knows what's happening," Feston said dismissively. "All the competent warriors went to Actondel, and the committees of the Caltatus know nothing but their statues and flowers. We will not find a suitable army here."

Verelli swore under his breath, though it was a predicament largely of their own doing. "Do what you can. We have to prevent any demons from escaping. We'll have our citadels in Mersania and Consarus do the same. Salvage anything possible but assume that everything within that area is expendable."

"You're talking about hundreds of thousands of people in that ring."

"I know," Verelli said.

There really wasn't anything to add. Unless the token king appeared with an uncharacteristic reserve of fortitude, the Conclave was likely the only remaining organization capable of holding the Reginum together. The last thing they needed was to waste themselves fighting for what was already lost.

"I'll do what I can," Feston said somberly, breaking the silence. "Where will you go?"

"Per the protocol, I'll make my way to Gramaria and hurry things along from there. Rydevan will have a good handle on what's happening in Actondel and know what our options may be."

"We have a fast ship waiting for just such a contingency. I'll see it readied for you before midnight. If anyone can hurry an army along, it's you."

Verelli hoped it would be so, even as he doubted the eventual effectiveness. Armies in the field had already proven to be ineffective against even a handful of demons and would likely continue to be so.

Or at least they would be, without the right defender.

* * *

It was late in the evening when the red-tile roofs of Gramaria at last came into view. The city was as yet untouched by those fleeing the carnage of Tythir, but there was no telling how long such placidity would last. Verelli stood impatiently at the rail as the small sloop tacked against the cold wind towards the docks. It was a position he had occupied almost the entire trip, as if his willpower alone could have sped his travels. They had sailed day and night without stop, bypassing any and every cluster of civilization they encountered to reach this, the farthest city from Tythir that was firmly under the Conclave's influence.

The captain guided the vessel unerringly towards an open berth, and the crew quickly tied the ship off.

The captain met Verelli at the gangplank.

"We'll be ready to sail again by morning," the captain said, eyeing the darkening streets. "Shall I send someone to escort you through the town?"

"My destination is only a short distance," Verelli answered. "I should be fine."

"As you say. There's fair enough more people scurrying about than I'd expect here this time of day. Something's got them stirred up, so keep an eye out for trouble."

"I will," Verelli promised.

He was thankful to finally disembark the cramped confines of the ship, and, though haste was in order, he resisted the urge to rush. Signs of overt panic were not visible on the faces of those around him, but there was a level of edginess to the actions of the crowd. News of what was happening had obviously reached the city, and he could only wonder what had changed in the days he had been aboard the ship.

The sun had fully set by the time he reached Rydevan's tower, and he pushed through the wrought-iron gates without slowing.

The walled courtyard was pleasantly lit by glowing stones of amber light, though it was empty except for a small garden. He was almost to the base of the tower when the door there opened, spilling bright light into the darkness. Silhouetted in the ruddy glow of the interior was a robed figure with a beard down to his waist and blue robes long enough to drag on the floor. Rydevan might look the part of a kindly hedge-wizard, but he had one of the sharpest minds in the Conclave.

"You look terrible," Rydevan said, his thick brows furrowed in concern.

"I'm famished," Verelli admitted. The boat had been well provisioned, but he had eaten little and slept less. There had been nothing to think about beyond the battles now being fought by everyone else, which only seemed to amplify his weariness.

"Come in, come in. We'll eat, and you can tell me just what in all the hells is going on."

Verelli allowed himself to be ushered inside, where servants took his cloak and wiped clean his boots. He was about to begin his explanation when he was interrupted by a small voice from behind.

"I got here as fast as I could."

Verelli turned to see Weeby leaning against a wall, so still that he had missed the diminutive halfling when he first entered.

"So did I," Verelli said, unsurprised to find him here already, even though Weeby's journey had been much longer than his own.

Rydevan waggled a finger at the halfling. "This little sneak showed up the day before your message and has availed himself far too freely of my hospitalities since then."

"He's just miffed that I knew you would end up here before he did." Weeby laughed, but his eyes never lost their worried expression. "It's bad, isn't it?"

Verelli took a deep breath, but there was no way to soften the news. "Tythir is lost."

Rydevan seemed to deflate at the proclamation. "We had feared as much. Let us sit."

He led them through an arched doorway into a cozy sitting chamber where comfortable seats awaited. Servants brought drinks and plates of warm breads and cool fruits. Verelli doubted he would be able to eat no matter how good it smelled, but his empty stomach quickly convinced him otherwise. Between mouthfuls, he filled them in on what he had seen and the decisions that had been made.

Rydevan shook his head when he was done. "We've always worried about an uncontained outbreak of this nature. I still can't believe the scale."

"I've voiced my warnings many a time," Verelli said. "You know my suspicions."

Rydevan sighed. "I do, and I share them, at least enough to have also forsaken the privilege of controlling a demon. I suppose I should thank you for that."

"Feston will probably try and use his as defense," Weeby observed. "He's always wanted to pit them against each other."

"I wish him the best," Verelli said, "but I would be leery of such experiments at a time like this."

"What do you intend now, old friend?" Rydevan asked. "Solor-Majalis must be retaken. Will you rally the lords to raise an army before returning east?"

"No," Verelli said with a shake of his head. "What we need is help, and not the kind that can be provided by common soldiers."

"So, you really intend to go through with it?" Weeby asked.

The question hung awkwardly in the silence that followed.

Despite the number of times he had considered the possibility, poking holes in every argument for and against until the logic rendered the decision inescapable, Verelli found himself reluctant to say it. It smacked too much of desperation.

Rydevan cocked his head to the side. "Go through with what?"

Weeby shook his head. "Oh, the irony of it all."

"What is this devious little imp talking about?" Rydevan's face grew worried. "You're not going to blow up my home again, are you?"

Verelli chuckled at the memory. "No, my friend, though that might be more palatable to us all." He stood and walked over to look out the window, wishing it would provide a glimpse of the future. "I'm going to find her."

"Who, Helen? Her aid would be invaluable at a time like this, but I believe she's terrorizing Westholm right now."

Weeby turned a disbelieving look on the elder wizard, one that perfectly conveyed his opinion of the man's intelligence.

"Oh," Rydevan said. "*That* her." His brows creased in concern. "You've shared your thoughts on the matter with me in the past, and I have kept them in the confidence the subject demanded, but there will be no hiding it if you do make the attempt. Your absence will be noted, particularly given what's happening, and some will call your loyalty into question. Even with all that you've told us, are things truly that bad?"

"I feel they are worse. When was the last time you received word from anyone in Tythir?"

Rydevan's shoulders sagged. "A week and a day."

Verelli nodded grimly. "The same morning I fled. If we do not act decisively, the entire Reginum might fall. If that should happen, there is no other kingdom on this continent that will be able to stand against a horde of demons."

Rydevan poured himself another drink. "Well, I can only hope you will return, with or without her, before this invasion reaches my doorstep. I shudder to think of even a handful of the creatures acting in unison outside of our control. If I had wanted to fight a war, I would have a sword over these robes."

"Oh, relax," Weeby said with a grin. "You know we'll be back before then."

"Says the overconfident one. Bring her here before the demons arrive, and I'll give you fifty gold signetas."

"Care to make it double if we get the elf girl, too?" Weeby asked with a wink and lopsided grin.

Rydevan rolled his eyes. "If either of them is as powerful as you've claimed, it would be worth it."

"Deal and done!" Weeby said.

Verelli almost laughed with him, but this gamble had far more than a coin purse at stake. "I don't know how long this will take," he cautioned. "I'm not even certain where she is at this point."

"She was off getting anointed," Weeby said, "or whatever the elves were going to do to her."

"Take the Gold Road to Merallin then?"

The halfling nodded. "It's a good place to start. With all the chaos in Actondel, she may well try to help her family stabilize their position. Maybe she'll even depose her useless father. Either way, if she's not there, we can work our way up the border."

"I will do my best to mask your leaving for as long as possible," Rydevan said, "though I make no guarantees."

"That's all I can ask of you," Verelli said. "I'll stay in

communication through the dohedron. Should the demons somehow break free and arrive here…"

"I will have the good sense to leave," Rydevan said. "And then I'll track you down and collect what your little friend owes me."

"Don't get your hopes up," Weeby shot back.

"Hope may be all we have soon, so I'll keep them as high as I can, thank you." Rydevan rose from his chair. "We should agree on a few things before you go, and we'll need to dust off some of those protocols. If you'll excuse me, I'll grab the books we need."

Weeby waited until the wizard had left before fixing Verelli with a piercing gaze. "Are you sure this is a good idea?"

For that, Verelli had no answer. Ceringion's military complement was scattered across the continent, Westholm was fractured and leaderless, and Actondel was on the brink of collapse. Seeking her amidst all that chaos might not be the wisest of decisions, but there was no other choice. Between the invading demons at his back and an angry holy warrior ahead, he could only wonder which of them would try to kill him first.

It is unfortunate that our visits to Eitholmir were so brief and contentious. The capital city of the elvish nation of Ildalarial is a wonderous place, one where nature and the steady craftsmanship of its inhabitants have intertwined so thoroughly that it can be difficult to tell where one ends and the other begins.

Yet it was anything but the warm and inviting place it first appeared to Shalindra. Hers was an uphill battle against tradition and desire, even though it was a conflict she constantly attempted to avoid. The forces that sought to hold her back were ultimately as doomed to failure as every other opponent who contested her destiny, and both the city and the people within were left better from her efforts.

Such shifts in perception are often a slow process, stretching across years or even lifetimes. Some changes, however, are as abrupt as they are far reaching. While Shalindra was responsible for her fair share of both, her most indelible impact was made when she was not even there.

An Avoidable Fate

The chamber from which the Grand Calontier ruled Ildalarial was ancient, older than the nation itself. The thick trees ringing its perimeter were joined together by wide panels of dark wood stacked atop footings of rounded stones. Curving windows broke each expanse at frequent intervals, brightening what might have otherwise been a gloomy chamber. Flowers and plants set beneath them brought additional cheer to the space, while the living canopy that formed the roof allowed in the sounds and fragrances of the forest.

Elothlirial smiled inwardly, every bit as confident in her position as Altalathlia here as she was within the temple forest's sacred glades. Given that fully half of the other ten counselors—Amalira, Valenia, Brialta, Yveralia, and Everiel—were Sisters of Elurithlia who answered to her in both realms, this was not surprising. The tradition of holding such dual leadership had waxed and waned over the centuries, but the past three Manalathlias had occupied both roles for the majority of their service. It was better that way, allowing Elurithlia's will to be delivered to the world through the actions of an entire nation.

Still, there were those even within Ildalarial who could not accept that wisdom. Jeverian's opposition to the evening's debates had been unexpectedly passionate and persuasive. His was a powerful family with a history of service to their nation almost as long as hers, but the river merchant could never see beyond the impact to his own enterprises. It was fortunate that she was here to keep him in check or he might have swayed the others into more short-sighted decisions.

Prosecuting a war against the weakened nation of Actondel was a necessary evil, but not one without some measure of justice. Atremiras, at least, saw the opportunity for what it was. His raiders had already seized or disrupted dozens of villages, the first steps in a campaign that would eventually reclaim all the lands lost to human expansion.

"As has been decided, so will it be," she said, dismissing them with the formal words, "and shall be spoken of forever with one voice."

"Forever with one voice," they echoed.

Following custom, the group remained silent as they began to file from the chamber. Atremiras lagged behind, waiting to gain her attention.

She paused to see what he wanted, and the other Sisters stopped with her. Jeverian's gaze lingered on them distrustfully from the doorway, but he made no comment.

"You may return to the temple," she said, waving the women onwards. "I will be along shortly."

Elothlirial was eager to hear the report that Atremiras had to give, but she wished he would learn to be more subtle in seeking her out. The soldier's face grew overly serious, as it always did when the news was good.

"Our Woodswardens confirmed that Actondel has taken almost their entire military eastwards, leaving only a token force to oppose us."

"I assume that you will press this advantage that Elurithlia has granted us and reclaim a sizeable piece of the lands stolen from us."

"Even against so light an opposition, we must not overextend," he cautioned. "We do not know the reason for this reallocation of their forces, beyond some general unrest in the east."

"More of their incessant infighting?"

"Perhaps. Regardless, we cannot guard the entire border or hope to lay an effective siege against their capital, and to be caught in the low country would spell disaster. Our opponents within this Calontier would be emboldened by any losses."

"I do not care what they think, as long as they continue to see the wisdom of supporting our efforts."

"And our goddess, Elurithlia?" Atremiras asked. "What does She say of all this?"

"She has offered no objections," Elothlirial said smoothly. She had also given no support, nor any other type of omen. Not since the heresy of the tainted Ascension.

"You know this campaign will be costly, and doubly so without the ability of your order to mend wounds and protect our minds. Actondel will not give up easily."

"My Sisters will accompany your men, as they always have," she replied, moving him towards the exit once more. "We have many skills."

"The loss of Her favor is an ill omen which affects morale. If there is any way we could display some favorable portent…?" He trailed off hopefully, but the goddess of the moon was not his to ask favors of.

"Our victories will be rewarded with a restoration of Her benevolence," she assured him. "See to that, and I shall ensure that She understands the depth of our resolve."

"Of course, Manalathlia." He bowed and left to his duties.

Elothlirial stood alone in the empty chamber, feeling the slightest pang of regret at the necessity of all the conflict. The humans had cost her so much—her happiness, her daughter, and even the favor of her goddess. It was time to repay that kindness.

* * *

Her resolve to see this invasion through was reinforced the next morning as she stood bathed in the harsh orange light cast by dozens of torches set upon poles in Lana Clariandar, the Glade of Worship. The flickering lights illuminated the desperation on the sea of faces that gazed up at her, waiting for the moment when she would lead them in the morning prayer. It was a ritual she had performed thousands of times, but always beneath the soothing coolness of Elurithlia's lights.

There were far more people here than usual, nearly matching the numbers found during the solstice celebrations. They brought with them an air of uncertainty and hopelessness—a thing not seen in this temple for generations. It was only with great effort that she kept her anger at the woman responsible for the situation from reaching her face, as any outward sign of displeasure would only exacerbate the angst of those who faced her now.

When the first rays of dawn brushed the treetops with their warm glow, she turned to face the east, feeling the ripple of sound as the faithful aligned themselves behind her. Closing her eyes and lifting her arms towards sky, she began to sing. Only those near this edge of the Glade would be able to hear her, but the words were known by all. Elation welled within her as the multitude of voices rose in chorus at her back. Such devotion would surely be rewarded, and to the words of the prayer she silently added her own unwavering commitment to victory over their enemies, in Her light. So fervent was her passion that she imagined she could feel Elurithlia's presence enter the Glade.

The sensation of someone moving close intruded on her prayer. Her first inclination was that Amalira had stepped in front of her for some reason, but an unexpected rush of warmth across the entirety of her body washed those thoughts away. It was no person who had come near her, it was a *presence*. Her eyes snapped open, and she beheld the outline of a shimmering figure standing before her: a woman of impossible grace wrapped in radiant moonlight and outlined with brilliant stars. Rapture flooded her heart. Elothlirial longed to fling herself into the arms of her goddess, but her body was no longer hers to control.

~ This assault should never have been allowed ~

The anger of those divine words struck her like a blow, piercing her mind with shards of ice and sending her careening sideways into Amalira.

~ See now what you have wrought ~

Elothlirial tumbled backwards across the grass as the warmth enveloping her surged to agonizing intensity. She cried out as her skin blistered and cracked, but there were none to hear her plea. The glade and everyone within had disappeared, consumed from one end to the other by a raging inferno that sprang up from nowhere. She grabbed desperately at her sacred symbol, the words of a protective prayer already on her lips, but the metal was so hot it melted the flesh from her fingers. Flaming trees toppled like wheat before the scythe as the ground trembled, and from within their once sheltering branches emerged an overpowering figure of myth and legend. It was a hideous, terrible monstrosity that loomed wickedly above her, a savage beast with wicked talons and cruel, piercing yellow eyes.

A demon.

Her naked terror propelled her like an arrow from a bow, flinging her high into the air. Elothlirial flailed helplessly as she hung suspended at the apex of her flight, witness to the scorched hellscape of heat and ash that engulfed the entire city. Then she was plummeting downwards into the towering flames. Past them she tumbled, crashing through the grass and dirt below until she emerged into the empty space beyond. Vertigo spun her vision in disorienting patterns, stopping only when she slammed face-first onto a windswept plain of harsh stony sand.

Staggering to her feet, she cast around for some frame of reference. Surrounding her now upon that forlorn plane were the worshipers from the Glade, all wandering about in a daze. She called out to them, barely hearing her own voice over the rush of the wind. One by one, their elvish bodies begin to twist and distort, ripping apart as they continued to swell. Their pitiful screams turned to snarls and growls as an endless swarm of demons took their place. Terrible caricatures of goats and wolves stalked in an ever-tightening circle around her. Above them all, gigantic winged beasts leered down at her helplessness in wicked delight.

Claw and stone, tooth and fist, their assault came at her from a thousand directions and yet nowhere all at once. Pain slashed through her mind as her flesh was torn away.

She begged her goddess for salvation, yet the calming touch that had sheltered her so many times remained unfelt, and she died over and over again.

The harsh violence of her ordeal ended so abruptly that Elothlirial wondered if the rustling of wind in the unburned trees was real or simply a final delusion of her dying mind as she left this world.

She lay once more upon the ground, this time with blades of grass instead of jagged stone pressing against her cheek. Shrieks and wails filled her ears, a cacophony of misery that was somehow more frightening than what she had just endured.

A voice—perhaps Avrilia's—rose above the din, sounding far away. "Care for those who are stricken! Comfort them as you can."

Gentle hands gripped her, easing her upright. Something cool was pressed against her forehead. She attempted to identify those who cared for her, but, open or closed, her eyes saw nothing but the afterimage of flaming destruction. It was only when she tried to speak that she realized she was one of the ones still screaming.

Elothlirial clamped her jaw shut, biting her lip until the salty taste of blood filled her mouth. She begged Elurithlia for strength, pleaded with Her for mercy, but such divine comforts remained out of reach. The terror gripping her eventually subsided, at last allowing her to regain control of her faculties.

As her vision returned, she was shocked to see that the two elves tending to her were not her fellow Sisters but a man and woman from the congregation.

"Help me stand," she commanded in a trembling voice.

They pulled her to her feet, continuing to regard her with concern. She wobbled but quickly withdrew from their attentions as she took measure of all about her.

The normally serene clearing lay awash in chaos. Small groups huddled together in prayer. Dozens, maybe hundreds, lay stunned or writhing on the ground. The frantic efforts of those rendering aid made it impossible to tell how many had been afflicted, but it was significant. The shadows, which had been retreating before the light of dawn, seemed to press back in, obscuring her vision.

The bedrock of her faith began to fracture beneath the crushing emptiness that descended upon her, and with it fled her remaining energy. She gripped the closest arm to prevent herself from sinking back to the ground. What it meant was well beyond any comprehension she could muster. All she knew was that something had gone terribly wrong.

* * *

That evening found an exhausted and dispirited group of Sisters cloistered within the Glade of Atonement. Their retreat to the private clearing within the temple forest had not been a reward for completion of their tasks; it had been forced on them by necessity. The shallow, oval reflecting pool in the center, edged by stones in perfect alignment with the phases of the moon, normally served as a mirror to their own thoughts, allowing careful contemplation of whatever issue might concern them.

Such was not the case today.

Elothlirial had never seen so many fearful expressions. Her Sisters were drained of their hopefulness and vigor, and she was well aware that her own haggard expression matched theirs. It had taken hours to first gather themselves and then attempt to calm those affected by the divine revelation, and even longer to convince them to return to their homes to rest. For every elf that departed the Glade of Worship, however, two more seemed to enter. Many wandered in on their own, others were carried in unresponsive by frantic relatives. They came desperate for comfort, yet there was none to give.

By noon, missives from the Grand Calontier had begun arriving, describing the ever-expanding crisis and requesting her answers in ever more stringent terms as the day marched on. She had ignored their demands, too focused on regaining command of the situation. By midafternoon the influx of the stricken had shown no signs of slowing. Elothlirial had at last ordered her inner circle to withdraw before they themselves became the patients.

She shook her head, struggling to focus on what needed to be done now. The message within that terrible vision had to be deciphered. Her mind shied away from every attempt, however, losing itself in the ruin of its aftermath instead. Such a lack of discipline was unbecoming, though she took some comfort in knowing that her Sisters were fairing no better.

Together they had prayed, and hoped, and fretted, but in the end, none of their theories had yielded a suitable explanation for the events of that morning. The silence of Elurithlia was again absolute, and it was left to their own minds to fill in the reasons why.

Brialta's sobs finally pulled Elothlirial from her musings, as the young cleric sank to the ground with her face buried in her hands. Valenia rushed to put her arms around her, looking just as frightened but perhaps finding solace in their shared grief. All of the women gathered around Elothlirial were every bit as confused and helpless as those looking to them for answers.

For once, she found the words she needed to say difficult to produce. "We have been given a sign," she began. "A message from our Mistress that cannot be denied. Do not fear what may come, for to show us these things means that She has given us the knowledge with which to avoid it."

They were good words that achieved the desired effect, but within Elothlirial's own mind, her world was crumbling faster than she could rebuild it, and her faith in herself wavered. They had to find some way to unravel the meaning behind what they had been shown, and so she began the search at the earliest beginning available to them.

"Avrilia? You alone remember the time of the last Guardian. Is there any precedent for such action?" Elothlirial had read the histories of that era and already knew the answer, but since the oldest woman present was one of the few not affected, it seemed a solid place to start.

Avrilia shook her head. "Never did anything like this happen. What you saw was more like the tales of Alta Amalia, of those who communed directly with our goddess and were granted visions of what was to be. But that was long ago."

"Shalindra received it," Brialta interjected. "Ennathalerial bore witness."

They could have done without the reminder of the human's warped Ascension and her own daughter's abandonment of her teachings. Disgust boiled in her stomach, but she did not have the strength to reply with any vitriol. Neither ceremony nor Guardian had been present within the nightmare.

"If not in the vision, there must be truth in Her words," she mumbled, almost to herself.

"What was that?" Avrilia asked.

"The words that were spoken during the vision," Elothlirial said, disliking the way everyone was looking at her.

"I heard no words," Amalira said.

Valenia shook her head as well. "Nor I."

"Did none of you hear them?" she asked, not believing that such strong and clear statements would not have been understood by all.

Her query was met only with worried stares.

Avrilia stepped closer. "What did She say to you?"

See now what you have wrought.

The haunting tones of that accusation echoed in Elothlirial's mind. If the words had been for her alone, it left the frightening possibility that it was only with *her* that Elurithlia was displeased. Was it the Ascension, then?

She had been opposed to a human assuming the role of guardian from the start, and this terrible vision might then serve as proof that she had been right.

Doubt wormed its way through that explanation almost immediately, no matter how much she wanted to believe it. The separation in time between the event and this warning were too great, and the vision had surrounded her with demons, not an impure Guardian.

The complete silence left her aware that everyone was waiting for her response. She was prevented from giving it as Amalira rushed into the glade. The senior priestess was frazzled almost to the point of being unkempt, and her face betrayed her discomfort with whatever news she carried.

"Forgive me, Manalathlia," Amalira said. "The Grand Calontier has convened an emergency session and requires our presence."

That was hardly a surprise. They were probably scared and desperate to appear to be doing something, when what was needed was for her to pursue these tantalizing lines of thought. It felt so close.

"Inform them that we will meet with them tomorrow."

Amalira wrung her hands. "I… Forgive me, but their demand was for us to appear immediately. There are Drisaniar outside."

The Drisaniar were guards tasked with the safety of all the members of the Grand Calontier. Though their duties were largely ceremonial—Ildalarial was a peaceful nation, unlike the human kingdoms to the east—they were the finest soldiers to be found anywhere.

"How kind of them to consider our safety," she said, projecting a calm demeanor while inwardly seething. This meddling by the Grand Calontier in affairs they were incapable of understanding was the last thing she needed. She turned back to Avrilia. "I will go and calm their distress. We must speak to everyone who saw the vision to discover not only what they saw but what they heard. Those of you who may not join me in council will assist. Discover every detail of this sign that Elurithlia has given us and look to the commonalities of who did and did not receive it."

"Yes, Manalathlia." Avrilia said it with confidence, but the old woman's eyes were filled with concern.

Elothlirial beckoned to Amalira and the other four women who belonged on the Calontier, and she led them away. The Glade of Worship remained full of people being tended to, and though no one called to her, the group's passing did not go unnoticed.

Members of their 'escort' awaited them just outside the temple forest in full ceremonial armor. Courtesies were exchanged and horses produced, but Elothlirial's thoughts had already drifted far away, and she went through the motions automatically. Had she truly been the only one to hear the message in the vision? And, if so, what did that signify? The possibilities swirled uncomfortably at the edges of her understanding as they rode through the city, yet she kept the brewing turmoil hidden behind a mask of confidence.

There was no disguising the armed escort whose protection was not needed, however, nor the unnecessary haste of horses for a route that could easily have been walked. Whispers and furtive glances followed them along the winding streets. The humiliation of the journey quickly blossomed into barely restrained anger, and when they reached their destination, she pushed her way ahead of the guards.

Conversation stopped as she stormed into the chamber of the Calontier. Her Sisters spread out behind her, and for a moment the two groups faced each other in silence. It was Jeverian who first addressed her.

"We are relieved you have at last joined us," he said. "Your absence at a time like this was cause for concern. Are you well?"

"I was busy," she sniped, in no mood for his games. "And this interruption does nothing but hamper our work."

"Perhaps you would benefit from the broader base of wisdom this Calontier can muster? Elurithlia's anger touched people across our entire nation."

As if she needed him to tell her that. He looked no different than he always did, far too composed to have experienced the vision himself. None of them, in fact, showed any signs of the emotional damage received by those who had seen it. There was nothing she could gain by being here, and made to end the charade as quickly as possible.

"If She is displeased, then it must stem from our decision to elevate a human woman—"

"That happened months ago," Jeverian countered. "The warning that struck down you and so many of your Sisters was unprecedented. The potential for hordes of demons sacking this city seems a good reason for us to consider alternatives to our current strategy."

Curse whoever had told him what they had been shown.

"I was attempting to decipher Her meaning when we were summoned here," she retaliated, not bothering to mask her ire.

The other counselors grew unwilling to meet her gaze. Jeverian, however, remained unaffected.

"Regardless of what your labor produces, it seems clear that now is not the time to prosecute a war against Actondel."

"We may never have such an opportunity again," Elothlirial protested, unable to understand why he thought this was relevant. "We agreed that—"

"What good will owning the old lands be if we lose Ildalarial in the process?" he demanded, his voice rising to match hers. "What will become of us when your hallowed temple is burned to ash? Assaulting Actondel's cities seems foolish when faced with our own ruin."

This assault should never have been allowed.

The words surged into her mind, blotting out her response.

Atremiras finally entered the debate, hotly contesting Jeverian's accusation, but their voices grew muffled as Elothlirial's memory of the vision overwhelmed her senses. She pushed past the burning flames and the smell of her own seared flesh, seeking where and how the words had been delivered. They were meant for every elf, surely. She wanted to believe it. She *had* to believe it.

And yet, she did not.

The prophetic horrors might have been granted to all, but the message… that had been for her ears alone. Her position as Elurithlia's most exalted servant upon this world could have explained it, of course. There was no one more suited as a conduit for Her teachings than the Manalathlia. Yet such rationalizations crumbled into excuses beneath even a casual examination. There was purpose in what had happened, as there was with everything her mistress did, and her own salvation hinged on her acceptance of what she had been told. The Ascension was her responsibility, no matter how tainted. The war with Actondel had many supporters, but she had manipulated the timing and manner of the attempt. No matter who else had contributed to Her ire, the resolution to those missteps could no longer be deflected. They would be her penance, and no other's.

She hung her head, fighting against the waves of guilt and shame crashing over her.

"Manalathlia?" Amalira's voice came to her, filled with concern.

Elothlirial looked up to find everyone staring at her, waiting.

"Do you agree to end the attacks on Actondel?" Kyleth demanded. "We are five for and five against."

"What is your answer?" Jeverian asked impatiently.

Elothlirial's hand drifted across the silver disc of her faith. She had led them astray, somehow. That was the answer. There was no denying it. In Her mercy, she had been shown her error and offered a chance at redemption. The only question now was how she would respond.

"I give no objection."

"Then I fear we must—" Jeverian paused, frowning. "What did you say?"

"We have displeased our goddess. Her dissatisfaction must be tended to with great care, and I would beg for time that I may work unhindered by the duties required by my oversight of this Calontier."

Amalira's mouth dropped open. Valenia clutched at her symbol, distraught. Even Atremiras' eyes were as wide as a startled deer's. They did not understand, and, in truth, Elothlirial did not either. But her mistress had not given up on her. Change was required, and, by Her light, she would be the one leading the realignment that was demanded.

Jeverian blinked, and, despite the bitterness at what she had just done, Elothlirial found the slightest amusement in his confusion.

Kyleth was first to respond. "We cannot be leaderless at such a time. I would call our vote to nominate Jeverian to the position of Altalathliar, with all enumerated titles and duties so prescribed."

It was smooth enough that it had probably been rehearsed. The power play was doubtless what the pair had been driving towards all along, no matter that it had been she who allowed them to succeed. It was an insignificant distraction compared to the calamity looming over them all. She raised her hand in agreement, and her Sisters reluctantly followed suit.

Jeverian cleared his throat. "Ah, I believe we are concluded with our business for the day. Thank you all for your confidence in me; and thank you, Manalathlia, for your wisdom. If there is any way we may assist your efforts, please allow us to do so."

She acknowledged his kindness with an inclination of her head, then led her dismayed Sisters from the chamber.

Once outside, Elothlirial brushed aside their looks of panic.

"They may have it, for now," she said. "It is to Her will that we must focus our efforts. Her words to me provide the key to our salvation, and proof that She has not forsaken us."

Her attitude seemed to reassure them, but she felt none of the confidence that she displayed.

They had failed, somehow.

Failed in their duties, failed in their devotion, and failed in their weakness. She would dig without mercy to locate the roots of those failures, be they within her temple or herself, and, by Her light, she would burn them one after another, until all was made right and pure.

Epilogue

An arctic blast of snow struck Fendrick hard in the face as he dove from the churning black mists of the portal, flash-freezing the sweat that drenched his body. He twisted in the air, cradling the unresponsive form of Alharania protectively in his thick arms. Their impact with the rocky ground almost jarred her loose, and they slid together through the snow until his helmeted head striking stone brought them to an abrupt halt.

"Close it!" he screamed, struggling to rise. Ellomir's aborted curse told him it was too late.

Energy snapped a hair's breadth above Fendrick's head with an audible report, its jagged arc vaporizing the falling snow into steam and burning an afterimage into his vision. The roar of pain behind him told that the wizard's aim had been true, even though it confirmed his worst fears. Battle cries echoed across the mountaintop as Verogin's soldiers rushed to his defense with sharpened spears.

Ellomir's beard whipped in the wind as he shouted his words of power, collapsing the portal to the demonic realm in on itself like smoke sucked into a bottle. In its place now stood a pair of the hulking, wolf-like demons whose savage pursuit had carried them through to this world at the last moment. Without hesitation, they fell upon their attackers.

Fendrick regained his feet, still clutching Alharania's slight elvish body in his arms, and cast about for a way to help.

"Get her out of here!" the wizard shouted at him.

He hesitated, knowing that the demons were far more than any of them could hope to handle without Alharania's protections.

Ellomir interposed himself between Fendrick and the monsters, his magic blasting one of the wolf-creatures in the face and knocking it back.

"Go!"

Fendrick ran, slipping and stumbling over the icy rocks as he raced desperately down the mountain. His breath came in ragged gasps that sent clouds of steam billowing in the air. He was poorly dressed for such frigid conditions after the extreme heat of the otherworld, and the bitter cold soon stole the feeling from his hands and feet despite the exertion of his flight. He did not slow, even as the terrain grew more jumbled and steep, forcing him ever closer to the cracked gorges cut by the river. The nearest cache of stores was half a day's walk, but they would both freeze should he take that long to reach it.

Suddenly, he was tumbling down a steep incline, never feeling the rock that tripped him. Alharania flew from his grasp as he hit the ground, leaving a bloody trail through the snow as she slid towards the jagged precipice. Fendrick scrambled after her on all fours, pulling her to a desperate stop just short of the edge.

An aborted scream chased his footprints down the forlorn

peak. The sounds of battle ceased, and all went silent save for the howling of the wind.

"Hold on," Fendrick pleaded with her. "I'll find a way out."

Alharania shivered uncontrollably, unable to make words come. Her cracked lips were now an ugly shade of blue, and the exposed skin of her arms was already changing to frighteningly unnatural colors.

Fendrick gathered her to him once more as he stood, but a glint of silver in the red-stained snow brought him up short. Shining Moon, the sacred warhammer forever paired with the silvered scales of her holy armor, remained where it had fallen. He reached for it instinctively, but his fingers had barely brushed the leather-wrapped grip when sharp daggers of pain stabbed up his arm. He jerked away.

"Why, Eluria!?" he cried. Was the whole world now turned against them? He cast a frightened glance over his shoulder as the all too familiar snarls of the demons grew louder, then turned back and spoke to the hammer as if it would understand. "Forgive me."

With a sharp kick, he sent the weapon spinning into the deep ravine. No matter how much they needed it now, he could not risk its loss to the demons.

Fendrick cradled her as gently as he could and ran in the opposite direction, desperately seeking a place to hide before they were either overtaken or froze to death. As if feeding on his terror, the snowfall turned heavy and fast, obscuring everything beyond a few paces and forcing him to navigate based on the contours of the mountain.

An unexpectedly steep downhill offered a barrier to the blowing wind, and the impenetrable white around him was replaced by the dark gray of stone to either side. The narrow cleft levelled off, coming to a dead end in a hollowed-out space that was open to the sky. A frozen pond covered almost the entirety of the floor, leaving no place to hide. He cursed at the bad luck and began to backtrack but stopped when he spied a darkened recess on the far side of the icy surface. Desperate for any respite, he inched his way along a thin ledge towards the opening, keeping Alharania's limp body towards the wall in case he should slip into the frigid water.

The darkened alcove revealed itself as the mouth of a cave, and he was forced to stoop to enter. After a short distance the ceiling rose to a more comfortable height, and he laid Alharania gently on the stone floor.

He inspected her damaged body carefully in the dim light, cataloguing every bloody claw mark and torn scale of armor, but even a cursory investigation would have revealed there was nothing he could do to heal them. He couldn't even defend her properly now, having lost everything beyond his armor and one short dagger.

Cupping her head gently in his hands, he begged her to wake.

Alharania's eyelids fluttered open. "It… is time."

"No!"

She raised a trembling hand towards his cheek, but her fingers reached no farther than his beard. "It was… already decided…"

Fendrick shook his head vehemently, as if the force of that action could deny what he knew he could not.

Alharania's body contorted, and she cried out in pain. "I am no longer whole!" She seized his wrists with sudden intensity. "You swore."

He bent close and pressed his lips to her forehead, unable to do it.

She pulled his fingers from her cheeks and onto her neck. "I do not fear the darkness," she whispered, "for it is there that Her light shines brightest."

Fendrick wept, but he would never go back on a promise made. Especially to her. He forced his fingers to tighten as he spoke the hated words, the dark and terrible phrases that churned like rancid meat in his bowels, ones that he had memorized under duress but had prayed he would never use. Searing pain coursed through his body as the dark magic took control, causing his skin to ripple and bulge and his bowels to empty. Fluids drooled from his mouth and nose and his vision blurred, but he fought to blink his watering eyes clear, determined to bear witness to the fate she was now consigned to. Alharania's mouth opened as she gasped for the air now denied her, yet even then she made no effort to stop what was being done. She twitched one last time as the light left her eyes, and the hand on his arm slid to the ground.

Fendrick shuddered, unsure if the waves of nausea sweeping over him were a sign that it had worked or simply a manifestation of his horror at what he had done.

Then an ethereal mist began to rise from her body, coalescing above her into a vaguely elvish shape before streaking away, deeper into the cave. He cried out a tortured apology, but it disappeared in the darkness.

His hand gripped his dagger, wishing for nothing so much as to plunge it into his own chest and die beside her, but such a merciful fate was now denied to him. Or at least he hoped it would be. His survival was the only thing that would bring worth to her sacrifice, but there was no reason to put it to the test against a pair of demons. Though his destiny was forever tainted by the scar burned upon his soul, he would not leave her there to be defiled.

He lifted her body, a bundle made somehow lighter without the spark of life within it yet unbearably heavy with the weight of his failure to keep her from this end. With a longing glance toward the darkened cavern where her spirit had fled, he crept slowly toward the exit and back out into the cold.

After circling the frozen pond and climbing back to the top of the crevasse, he paused to listen.

The wind had slowed, but the angry search of the demons was apparent, their rage bouncing like hurled stones between the rock walls of the mountains. Another sound, that of rushing water, offered him some hope that he had not strayed too far from their original course. If he could make it across the river, he might be able to elude the demons and locate one of the caches the group had left for the return trip. The demons were far too large to pass the way he intended to travel, and they would almost certainly freeze before finding another way around.

He made a dash down the rocky slope, slipping and falling over and over until his knees were bloodied and raw. Alharania was beyond such pain now, but he protected her from those falls every bit as much as if she were still alive. He was almost down the steep incline, within sight of the river crossing, when a roar from behind told him that the demons had picked up his trail.

Running now without any thoughts of stealth, he sped towards the thunder of the waterfall. The crossing he sought was only steps from that precarious edge, where the river plummeted over the side of the mountain. It had taken the entire group working together to ford the river safely, but now there was only him.

A glance over his shoulder showed him the nightmare of both massive beasts tearing through the snow on all fours. He plunged into the river without slowing. The rushing water was so cold it shocked his breath away and left his legs numb before even the fourth step. The force of the current pushed him closer to the edge, threatening to hurl him to his doom. If he could just reach the ledge on the other side…

The first demon slid to a stop at the water's edge, howling and snapping. It reached for him with long arms, its dagger-like talons swiping the air, but it was unwilling to enter the water.

For a moment, Fendrick felt a spark of hope that his plan would succeed, but then the second demon launched itself outward from the slope above. Fendrick ducked, nearly submerging himself in his effort to dodge, but the beast's trajectory sent it sailing well past him. It landed just short of the far shore with a tremendous splash. Howls of pain filled the air as it scrambled from the water, thrashing about upon the shores as if burned.

Fendrick stopped, caught between the two demons in the middle of the freezing river. This day would see no shred of victory. All he could do now was rob them of theirs. Clutching Alharania's body tight against his chest, he lifted his feet and allowed the waters to take them.

The demons bellowed in impotent fury as he was swept away. Fendrick's stomach left him as they were flung over the precipice and into the empty air beyond. He plunged towards the rocks miles below, praying the entire way down that he would not live to face the consequences of the evil he had done.

* * *

The echoes of that terrible day centuries ago still lingered in the air as Fendrick stood staring once more at that thundering waterfall. He would never be able to escape the past, but he could draw comfort from the fact that, with Shalindra's triumph over the demon goddess, no one else would ever be consigned to repeat it.

Forcing himself from those dark memories, he approached the water's edge. This time, he was well-protected from the cold and from every creature that could have stood in his way, but the clothing and weapons he carried would serve him no good against the rushing river. There was no Guardian to carry him unharmed across those turbulent waters this time, and no wizards to warm him with hot tea afterwards. He was truly alone in this endeavor, as he had been seemingly forever.

"Best to get on with it," he muttered to himself.

He located a promising spot between a pair of large stones and built a small fire there, sheltered from the wind. Once it had burned long enough to produce hot coals, he swept the smoldering embers into a clay jar with holes cut around the bottom and near the lid. The wind swirled snow around him, but he barely noticed as he pulled off his boots and both pairs of socks. The socks he stuffed down his coat where they would remain warm against his chest. He checked and rechecked every strap and buckle on his pack, then situated it as high on his shoulders as it would go, with the precious jar of embers on top. As ready as he could be, he returned to the water's edge.

Using his spear for balance, he set his first foot into the river. No matter how well he had prepared, the sting of the frigid water forced an involuntary gasp from his lips. By the time he was ten steps out, he had already lost feeling in his toes. The strong current tugged at him, waiting for any mistake. He forced himself to go slowly, measuring the depth with the butt of his spear before every step.

Not halfway across, the waters became too deep, and he was forced to backtrack, cursing the shifting rocks through his chattering teeth. Two more routes he tried, and after abandoning both he was left closer to where he had entered than the far shore he needed to reach. Half his body was so numb it was beginning to feel warm and he despaired at the possibility of giving up to try again later.

Committing himself to one final attempt, he returned to his original path. The water became deep enough once more that he began to lift from the bed of the river, but this time he pushed off hard with his spear like a bargeman. He floated helplessly for one panicked moment before being driven into a cluster of rocks beneath the surface. He wedged his feet between them, wondering as he did so why he could hear Verelli and Shalindra encouraging him to push on. The next thing he knew, he was stumbling from the water, delirious to the point that he could produce no memory of the latter half of his crossing.

Achieving the far bank only exchanged one danger for another, as the breeze chilled him even worse than had the water. He left a soggy trail as he teetered stiff-legged towards a protuberance of rock large enough to cut the wind, then collapsed behind it. The uncontrollable shivering wracking his body nearly prevented him from shedding his pack, and it was only with excruciating slowness that he freed the jar and the oilcloth-wrapped bundle secured atop it.

He clumsily brushed a dry spot in the snow, then unrolled the cloth and dumped the dried sticks within onto the ground. His teeth chattered violently, and his arms shook with such intensity that, when he tried to empty the burning embers onto the sticks, he almost missed.

Curling into a fetal position around the pile, he blew upon it as best he could to coax the fire to life. His eyelids grew heavy as he stared at the burgeoning flames. An eternity crawled by as the fire slowly grew and hints of warmth crept into his fingers. Still shivering, he set a small pot filled with snow directly on the fire, then worked to pull dry socks and boots over his ice-encrusted feet.

When steam began to issue from the pot, he gulped down the boiling liquid straight, without benefit of tea leaves. It scalded his tongue, but, as the heat seeped into his bones, he did not care.

Finally warmed enough to function, he pushed himself upright. The light was already fading, and it would not do to be caught here in the night, not when he was so close.

Though he had no plans to use them, he gathered all the fresh embers into the fire pot once more and pushed his tired body into motion. It was a short but steep climb to reach his destination, and it was almost dark by the time he finally located the fissure in the rock. With haste, he followed it downward, skirting the frozen pond that still filled the floor.

Only when he was within the cave did he at last breathe a sigh of relief. The embers within the fire pot retained enough heat for him to light a torch without resorting to flint and steel, and while the meticulousness of his nature demanded that he construct another fire just in case, his eagerness drove him onwards without the precaution. He paid no mind to the ancient figures and symbols painted in ochre along the cave walls—the knowledge and schemes of the gods no longer occupied his concerns.

So much had happened in the few months since his last visit that it almost seemed a lifetime ago and somehow less recent than the first time he had set foot here. He made his way down through the cave, disabling the magical wards he had left as he went, until he at last reached the subterranean lake.

Alharania was waiting for him, floating silently above the mirrored surface of the water.

He shed the items of this life as he approached, and she drifted closer to the shore, matching his pace.

His spear clattered to the stones first, then his pack, followed by his hood and hat and gloves. As his coat hit the ground behind him, Fendrick reached into his vest and withdrew a small ornately carved wooden box—the same one that Father Nathan had presented him with years ago, though the priest could never have guessed at the value of what it contained. It was Shalindra, not himself, who had at last filled it with all that had been lost, though the how of it all mattered less and less with every step he took.

Alharania's eyes lit up as he opened it and held it forth.

The glow that emanated from within the tiny container eased the harsh lines of pain from her haggard features. Neither of them took an action nor gave a command. The glowing shards of her stolen life escaped like butterflies into the air, seeking their own return to where they belonged. She welcomed them into herself, one after another, every reunion producing a brilliant flash of light that sparkled like stars throughout the cavern and stirred the waters of the lake. Her translucent countenance softened, slowly resuming the youthful appearance that she had possessed in life.

As the last flickers of light faded, Alharania leapt forward and wrapped her arms around him. He clutched her tightly, rejoicing at the touch of her embrace for the first time in hundreds of years. Her joyous laughter, free of judgement or blame, banished the enormous guilt he had labored beneath for so long, releasing a joy within him that he had thought lost.

His body was falling to the stones behind him, but Fendrick no longer cared. They were, at last, as they were meant to be, and the centuries of pain they had endured melted into memory like snow before the light of a new day.

MEET THE AUTHOR

David A. Godwin was born in Tennessee, during a simpler era when daydreaming was still allowed. Though successful in a number of more practical pursuits, he prefers to spend his time exploring made-up worlds filled with magical creatures and endless possibilities, and is often observed in deep conversation with his imaginary friends.

VISIT THE AUTHOR AT

www.dagodwin.com

for

The Latest News

Upcoming Releases

Exclusive Content